MY FRIENDS, MY CHOSEN FAMILY

MY FRIENDS, MY CHOSEN FAMILY

by Kyle Scafide

For Steve

Table of Contents

Introduction

The genesis of this book goes back to the 1990s, which is when I wrote the bulk of the narrative. At the time, I was editor-in-chief of *IMPACT* and *eclipse*, two bi-weekly LGBTQ publications that had been serving New Orleans and the Gulf South region for many years. While in the process of creating new content for *eclipse*, we decided that it would be fun to include a series involving recurring, fictional LGBTQ characters who lived in New Orleans.

The idea was not an original one. I was (still am) a big fan of Armistead Maupin's *Tales of the City*, which began as a series of installments printed in the *San Francisco Chronicle* in the late 1970s and into the 80s. Even though my publications were much more humble than the *Chronicle*, I thought that it would be a good idea to serialize a book in much the same way as Maupin did.

The series was a success. After a few months of installments, people began to stop me in the street and ask questions about the characters. I would hear things like, "Oh, I was so excited to hear about Joel!" Or "Jerry reminds me of my landlord!"

And then, of course, there were the people who would pump me for information about what was going to happen. "Don't leave me hanging! What is Barry going to do?" Or "What's going to happen with that closeted married guy who was cruising Audubon Park? Is he going to be a regular?"

And so on and so forth.

Time passed. I sold the publications in 1998, and life moved on.

When I stumbled onto the work many years later, it was like finding a much-loved high school scrapbook in a dust-covered box in the attic. I began to read it, and I found it hard to put down. It was not only the lovable characters who enthralled me, but also the experience of being transported back to 1990s New Orleans.

I tried to put it out of my mind. Sometimes, the stories would meander back into my consciousness, but I would dismiss any thoughts of revisiting the work, assuming that it would be outdated and not worth the trouble.

After I'd finished my first novel and was hitting a wall about halfway through the second, I decided to dust off this manuscript to see if that would reignite some creativity. I still wasn't convinced that I was ready to commit to the job, but I enjoyed the characters so much that I decided to do some editing to see what would come of the effort.

When I finally made the decision to consider this work as a novel, I assumed that I would need to rewrite the entire book so that it was contemporary; however, as I lost myself in the storyline, I felt like I was magically transported back in time to the '90s. I loved the feeling. I decided that my readers might also enjoy a peek at this literary time capsule, so I left the milieu alone.

For a number of reasons, there are significant revisions from—and additions to—the original. For example, there were redundancies that needed to be addressed. In its initial incarnation, this work was intended to be meted out in installments, much like Maupin's *Tales of the City*. In each published issue, I had to weave reminders into the prose to reintroduce a character who had not appeared for a while. In novel form, these reminders were no longer necessary, so I believe that I was successful in weeding out most of these pesky redundancies. Also, I added sections here and there to allow better flow and to make the narrative more seamless.

Next, I realized that the story had good bones but not much muscle, so I spent some time writing additional vignettes and editing the bits that needed it. After consulting with industry experts, it was suggested that the work was too long and that I should consider publishing about half of it as a shorter novel that could be offered at a reasonable price. The last thing I realized was that there was no ending at this halfway point, because it was intended to be an ongoing work. (Again, much like Maupin's *Tales*). Hence, I added a scene that gives some closure to the book, but it is also open-ended so that—if I earn encouragement from pleased readers—I can consider the possibility of publishing another volume.

I'll be honest and say that this was never intended to be a serious work of literature. It's light, enjoyable reading. If you're looking for Steinbeck or Proust, you won't find them here. You can read one of my other novels if you're looking for something more serious; however, if you want a story that will always keep your attention and that is filled with lovable characters who will make you want to move to New Orleans (or never leave), then this book is for you.

I hope you enjoy reading it as much as I enjoyed writing it.

Joel & Lance

Joel couldn't believe he had gotten into this predicament again. Lance just didn't seem capable of sensing his discomfort, and Joel knew from past experience that this badgering was going to last some time. He prepared himself for the next onslaught.

"C'mon, man, she really likes you," Lance pleaded, resting a muscular shoulder against the door jamb. "We'd have a great time, I promise."

Joel leaned back in his computer chair. "Look, it's not that I don't want to go, but man, I've got these two papers to do, and I just don't have the time this weekend."

Lance frowned and rocked gently back and forth against the door, plotting his next offensive argument. He reminded Joel of his friend Wayne, who used to lollygag around his house when they were twelve years old until he finally convinced Joel to get his nose out of a book and get outside to play some ball. Come to think of it, Wayne had blond hair too.

Lance's eyebrows lifted, and his blue eyes began to widen.

Uh oh, thought Joel. He could tell that Lance had conjured up a new line of attack.

"Okay, tell you what," reasoned Lance, "you can skip the movie part and we'll pick you up on our way to the Saloon about eleven. And please don't tell me you'll still be writing that late."

Joel's inner voice cursed him. If anything, he would have preferred going to the "movie part" and skipping the goddamn Water Hole Saloon. Being out late was always the hardest part, because then all the pressure was on to take her back to her apartment, smooch at the door or, he feared, bury the bone. He'd have to get out of this somehow.

"Lance, man, I want to get to bed early so I can get up in the morning and get started again. You know if we go out we'll end up staying there until at least 2 a.m. Or later. I just can't do it man, really."

This time, Lance came up with a compromise without having to think about it.

"Okay, then take your own car and just meet us at the Saloon. The movie gets out at about ten thirty, so we should be there no later than eleven, unless we can't find a parking spot."

Joel couldn't help smiling just a little. The last time that Lance had cajoled him into going to the Quarter with him, Lance had to pee really bad, and it took them so long to find a parking spot that, out of desperation, he jumped out at a corner on Burgundy Street and peed on a gate next to a house. Right about the same time Lance exclaimed "AHHH, that feels great," a German Shepherd leapt at the gate, barking. Lance had been so taken by surprise that he fell backwards, landing first on his butt and then his back, with the last trail of piss landing on his pants, his cock still hanging out. Joel had jumped out of the car, laughing hard, but it wasn't really to help Lance stand up as much as it was to get a closer look at what was banging around outside of his jeans.

Ahh, memories…

Joel looked up and saw a puzzled look on Lance's face, and it wasn't until then that he realized he had laughed out loud.

"I'm sorry, Lance, I was just picturing you scared shitless and pissing all over Burgundy Street…and yourself!"

Lance smirked at him. "Hey, I pissed, didn't I?"

"Yea, all over yourself." Joel got caught up in the camaraderie, and before he knew what he was saying, it came out. "Okay, dammit, I'll meet you there at about eleven, but I dunno about this Wendy thing. I just met her a coupla times, and you're always trying to set me up."

Lance stood straight up, his muscular torso enhanced by the tight green tee shirt he had on. Joel was beginning to think that the "t" in tee shirt stood for Tulane, since so many students had nothing else in their wardrobe. It was a lot different from the formal attire at the Catholic high school he had attended before going to college.

"Look," said Lance, taking a firm stance with his arms crossed, trying to look concerned. "If you don't get out more, I'm gonna see to it that you're committed to a monastery."

Joel grinned. He thought for a moment about that prospect. Maybe it wouldn't be so bad. He heard that you could get a lot of action there.

"You don't have to worry about me, thank you very much. I'm just really trying to concentrate on my studies. I guess not everybody can be as lucky as you and not have to study."

Joel immediately regretted saying it when he saw Lance's face shift to a look of fear—a subtle change, but Joel recognized it.

"I'm sorry man, I didn't mean to make fun, really." Lance had goofed off a lot during his freshman year, and when his father heard about the three "Cs," he really chewed Lance's ass.

"That's alright, man, I know I need to study more. But shit, I've been bustin' my butt all week, and hell, it's Saturday night. A guy's gotta get some action, you know?" He smiled down at Joel, who had just realized that he had gotten duped into yet another long evening of discomfort.

Joel tried to be convincing. "Yea, I guess so. I can't wait."

Yeah, right, he thought to himself, sighing and leaning back in his chair.

I can't wait until this evening's over.

* * * *

Barry

"This one rents for $500 a month, plus deposit." Jake took a long drag on his cigarette and leaned back out the front door shutters to blow. Barry nodded and walked into the next room, which turned out to be the *only* other room.

Jake blew another cloud of smoke outside, so the next sentences came from a distance, like he was tired of making the effort to be understood.

"It's amazing how rents have gone up in the Quarter this past year or so. Used to be, a few years ago, early '90s, a place like this went for less than $400 a month, believe it or not."

Barry couldn't believe it. But at least it was better than where he had lived in Dallas. The one bedroom apartment he had shared with his ex went for the same amount, but it was nothing more than an apartment in an apartment complex surrounded by other apartment complexes. At least this apartment had some originality, if nothing else. He leaned back into the first room.

"Have anything else you can show me?"

A look somewhere between frustration and downright disgust appeared on the agent's face. More smoke out the door.

"Not in this range." He seemed to be giving up on the idea of trying to make himself heard. "If you want, we can take a look in the Marigny. You know, right outside the Quarter."

Barry considered this prospect for a moment, but he admitted to himself that he really wanted a place in the Quarter. After all, that's where pretty, newly single, thirty-something gay men are supposed to live, right? He smiled to himself and re-entered the kitchen/dining/living room.

"You mind if we turn on the ac?"

"Not at all, if the electric's on." There was a brief, clumsy silence until it dawned on Jake that he was supposed to do something.

"Oh, uh, let me get it," he mumbled. Holding on to the doorframe with his left hand, he stretched all the way out the door, flinging his cigarette butt, barely missing a car that was speeding down Dauphine Street.

Barry took a closer look at the bricked-up fireplace and the mantle above it then continued his slow meandering around the apartment. He had to go slowly; he was running out of apartment to look at, and soon found himself right back where he started.

As he turned away from the mantle, he could see Jake stretching to turn on a window unit in the upper half of the window. As his fingers fumbled with the buttons, more and more of his shirt pulled out from his pants, revealing a sizable middle-age paunch above his belt, and Barry stifled a grin when he saw the tattered upper edges of what appeared to be blue polka-dotted underwear. Jake muttered something about trying to find the right button, and immediately a loud but brief vibrating noise rattled the windows until the motor reached its peak. Jake grunted as he let his arms down. When he turned around, he was smiling like he had just solved world hunger.

Almost caught in the act of shirt tail-peeking, Barry shifted his gaze to the refrigerator.

"This come with the apartment? Plus the stove and the window units?"

"Oh, yeah, that's included in the rent." Jake tucked away his precious polka dots. "Most of the apartments in the Quarter have appliances. How well they work, well, that's another thing." He let out a "whew" like the task with theAChad worn him out. "Did you take a look at the bath yet?" He walked to the bedroom, still adjusting his attire.

"Not really." Barry was looking in the kitchen cabinets, trying to figure out if his dishes would fit there. He closed the cabinet doors and made his way to the bedroom. "I took a peek, but it was too dark. I couldn't find the light switch."

"Well, I think I can manage that," answered Jake, who began feeling along the walls of the bathroom. "Oh, I shoulda figured." There was a scraping sound, and light poured out of the bathroom.

"Should've figured what?"

"Well, it has a pull chain over the sink. I guess they decided not to change this charming little feature when they did the renovation."

Barry stepped in for a closer look, blocking the doorway as he did so. He noticed Jake seemed a little nervous.

"Here, uh, let me get outta your way, so you can get a better look." Jake looked downward and sidled past him through the door. Barry had been told many times that his green eyes were disarming, so he had grown accustomed to people stammering when they locked eyes with him.

"So what do you think?" asked Jake.

Barry hesitated, knowing that this could be the "I've finally got you" question. He had to admit it wasn't a bad apartment, even if it was a bit small. And compared to some of the dingy, musty smelling places he had seen so far, this was a steal. He walked back to the front room.

"I guess it's okay."

Jake didn't seem pleased with that response. "You know," he said, following Barry like an injured child, "you've had a chance to see everything in this price range in the Quarter. Don't you think this would do? And after all, you could always move after a year, if you found a better place."

Barry stopped at the open counter that separated the kitchen from the rest of the room and pulled himself up to sit down, his strong arms performing this feat effortlessly.

Jake grinned. "Tired of walkin', huh?"

Barry shrugged as he looked over at the agent, feeling a little sorry for him. After all, he had dragged the guy around the Quarter for the better part of the afternoon, and in September in New Orleans, that kind of dedication deserves commendation.

"Yeah, I bet you could use a break too." Barry moved over, inviting Jake to sit.

"Well, I guess you're right." Jake's grin was usurped by grunting as he hoisted himself up to the countertop a couple of feet away from where Barry was sitting. "I hope this counter can take all this weight."

Barry smiled and let out a single "hmph." Despite Jake's outdated clothes and his slightly goofy nature, he was a nice enough guy, though he seemed depressed underneath it all. Barry imagined that his own brown hair would be turning gray soon enough, when he was in his forties.

A period of blissful silence ensued as they basked in the cool sensation of sweat evaporating from their foreheads. It was Barry who broke the silence.

"Okay, let's go for it."

Jake beamed in triumph and jumped off the countertop.

"Okay, then! Why don't we get back to the office and do the paperwork? I need to turn off the lights and stuff first." He stretched up toward the ac, and out came the polka dots again.

* * * *

Joel toweled himself off, his skin tingling from the cold rush of air on his damp skin. He threw on his bathrobe while he dried his hair, trying to figure out how he was going to pull off this little "date" as painlessly as possible. He looked at the clock and saw that he needed to hurry.

"Damn!" he said out loud, falling on his bed and staring at the ceiling. He was so angry with himself for giving in to Lance's wishes.

"I'm so lonely," he whispered to himself. The ceiling above him went dim as his eyes watered up. He blinked hard. No, he thought, I'm not going to cry.

He sat up, resting his hands on either side of him and rubbing the carpet with his toes.

What was it like to go out with a guy? Just the idea made his heart beat faster. *God, what would Lance do if he found out that I had the hots for him?* In spite of his mood, Joel had to smile at the thought.

He stood up, threw on a pair of underwear and walked toward the full-length mirror hanging behind the door. This was the closest he had ever come to another naked man. Ignoring the view of his face, Joel studied his body from the neck down, imagining another man there— a man like him, with a small patch of hair on his chest and a thin line of hair…The response to his fantasy was a rise in his briefs.

God, it would be great to be with another guy who would look me in the eye with love on his mind.

Joel looked up at his dream man, but all he saw was his own face, his own deep brown eyes filled with longing.

"This is creepy," he mumbled. His passion subsided, replaced by utter loneliness.

Will I ever find a man to love me? When?

One day, he thought.

Maybe one day.

* * * *

Linda & Patricia

"All right, ladies, none of this farting around. According to my watch, you've got a good twenty minutes of work to do before you get outta here. So get to it."

Jeez, thought Linda, ol' man Taormino could be such an ass. She stuck out her tongue, which he pretended not to see as he lumbered out of sight. She looked at her watch. 4:40. Twenty minutes was an eternity on Friday afternoon, especially since she was looking forward to it for a change.

Two of her friends were going to meet her at The Mint for a few drinks, after which they would undoubtedly stagger out for a bite.

She found herself staring out into space, but at the sound of Asshole's approaching footsteps, she hunched over the pile of paperwork on her desk, making notes for attorneys who were either too stupid or too lazy to do it themselves. A career as a paralegal had seemed so exotic to her when she was in school. They forgot to mention that she would actually have to work with—rather, for— asshole attorneys.

Once again, his large figure seemed to absorb light when he walked into the room, but this time he just peeked and went away. Linda looked across the office at Betty, hard at work in her own cubicle. She discreetly studied the fifty-year-old woman's tireless work method. The only break in stride came when she reached for those long menthol cigarettes she smoked. Her face would almost disappear for a moment as she blew the smoke away. When it cleared, there she was, pecking away on her word processor, totally oblivious to the world.

Linda shook herself back to reality, checking her watch one last time before she went back to work.

Fifteen minutes. Damn.

Looking back at the computer screen, she reached for the mouse, thinking she could easily kill this time doing some spell-checking and editing. She did not want to dig into any more dusty books this afternoon.

"How's the research coming?"

Linda jumped.

"Oh, hi, Steve." She found her hand on her chest. "You scared the hell out of me."

"C'mon," he smiled, leaning over her desk. He looked around to make sure that there were no passersby and whispered, "It's only the old fart who's supposed to scare people around here."

Betty stirred from her stupor long enough to pipe in. "Hey, don't get her started. She's been sassy all day."

"That's why we hired her, Betty." Steve straightened up and walked away, adjusting his tie and shouting over his shoulder, "She's supposed to really tick us off before we go to court. Right, Linda?"

"Right!"

Thank God for Steve, she thought. Even though he is an attorney, at least he's a friendly one. His being gay was a plus, as well. When Linda came out after being divorced for two years, it was Steve who stood by her, defending her whenever she screwed up.

Lord, I sure screwed up a lot.

Her mind began to drift, and painful memories of rejection began to resurface. In general, the African American community had a difficult time accepting homosexuality. After her divorce, she had been counseled by her parish priest, who also helped her parents through the most difficult period after her coming out. The relationship with her father, especially, was still strained from that ordeal. She recalled the hell she had been through with Jan, her first lover. It was hard enough admitting she was a lesbian, but having to admit that she had shacked up with a loony toon was too much. She managed to get through it, thanks to people like Steve and Patricia.

Oh, sweet Patricia.

Linda managed to focus on her work for a while, but she began to put away her files as soon as she heard Betty bustling at her desk, packing up her purse. Those sounds were more trustworthy than any five o'clock whistle.

"Oh, finally," said Linda, shutting down her Mac. "I was going bonkers." She reached for her purse and retrieved her cosmetic bag for a last-minute touchup, then began applying bright red lipstick. She was barely audible as she asked, "What are you and John up to this weekend?"

Not looking up from her task, Betty mumbled, "Same ol'. If we can stand the heat, we may take the boat out on Sunday. Other than that…" Betty was already headed for the door, seeing no need to complete her sentence.

"Have a nice weekend, hon," she yelled back, stopping long enough to wink and say, "Don't do anything I wouldn't do."

Linda wondered if she noticed her cheeks blush. She recovered fast enough to get cocky and yell back, "I'm planning on doing things *no* one would do." She started to add "with Patricia," but regaining her senses, she grabbed her keys and ran out before Asshole could catch her.

* * * *

The Mint was not crowded when Linda arrived at about 5:15. She was a little early, because she had lucked out with a good parking spot.

Tad was waiting behind the bar. "Hey, honey, what's up?" Tad's close-cropped hair seemed to glisten as he gave his cheek to Linda, who leaned over the bar and exchanged air kisses with him.

She pursed her lips on either side of his face. "Mwah, mwah."

"Honey, that's the best action I had all week," said Tad, smirking as he threw a small towel over the condiment tray. "Too bad you're not a fireman."

Linda laughed. "Tad, you are tooooo much." She picked up the towel and threw it at him.

"Watch it girlie, it's too early to start any shit. And leave that towel there. If I don't cover up those cherries and olives, your dyke friends will come in here and think it's the all-you-can-eat salad bar. So whatcha havin'?"

"Okay, okay. Gimme a Cape Cod."

Tad swished to the other end of the bar to get cranberry juice, abusing his customers along the way.

Linda took a seat at the bar and began to reminisce. It had already been three years since she had come out of the closet and started coming to the Mint. She stared out the windows facing Decatur Street, recalling those memories.

"Wake up, girlie, and give me some money."

Linda turned to see Tad with one hand palm up and a drink in the other.

"It is still Happy Hour, isn't it?"

Tad rolled his eyes. "Yes, missy, it's cheap, if that's what you mean."

Linda laughed and fished a five out of her purse.

"You sure you're a lesbian? I ain't seen a lesbian with a purse before."

"You expect a tip with this kind of abuse?"

"Oh get off it, honey," he snapped, grabbing the bill out of her hand. "I'm just gettin' warmed up."

Off he sashayed to get her change. There was a small commotion at the door behind her, and Linda turned to see two women embracing in the doorway. It was Patricia and Dottie, who had arrived at the same time.

The two were still chatting when Patricia glanced over to see Linda looking at them.

"Oh, hi Linda!" Patricia beamed, cutting off Dottie in mid-sentence. "Been here long?"

"No, just a few minutes," she answered, giving Patricia a warm hug. "And how's my favorite roommate doing?" she asked, giving Dottie a hug in turn.

"Okay," she replied. "Oh, the reason why Patricia and I were laughing when we came in was because she asked me how work was, and I forgot the name of the hospital!"

This brought a round of laughter from all three of them. Dottie worked in the admitting department of Baptist Hospital, but the name had changed twice in the last two years due to mergers.

"Sometimes I wish I could completely forget about work," said Patricia.

"Me too," chimed in Linda. "Or at least forget the asshole that makes my life a living hell."

"Well, that's what bars are for, right? Forgetting?"

As Patricia said this, she pulled her hair back with both hands and let it fall behind her shoulders.

Hmmm, thought Linda as she locked eyes with Patricia.

That's what you're for.

* * * *

Jerry, Philip, & Darlene

Jerry was dripping with sweat once again as he dragged the sprinkler to another part of the yard. He wasn't sure if the water dripping off of his balding head was due to the heat or the dysfunctional sprinkler he was using.

"Hey, old man, can't you hire people to do that?" Jerry looked up to see one of his tenants walking toward him from the street. "After all, a southern lady of your age should at least have on a big, floppy hat."

Jerry straightened up from his stooped position, groaning as he scurried to avoid the oncoming spray of water. "If you look this good when you're sixty…"

"Oh, is it still sixty? I could have sworn we celebrated that birthday years ago." Philip plopped down on a lawn chair on the patio, but soon realized his mistake when the sprinkler managed to wet his shins. "Shit!"

Philip dropped his briefcase then tripped over it as he made a desperate retreat from the sprinkler. Jerry laughed so hard he had to lean on the wall of the patio.

"It's not nice to fool with mother landlord," taunted Jerry. "Are you okay?"

Philip nodded as he picked up his briefcase. Jerry watched him lovingly, gratefully. He was so happy with Philip and his other tenant, Darlene. If only he could have had a gay role model when he was Philip's age.

Philip scowled as he examined his wet suit pants. "It's been awhile since I wet my pants." Looking up, he added with a smile, "Outside, that is."

"You're twisted." Jerry began walking toward him, keeping out of the sprinkler's territory. "Speaking of wetting pants, how are the little boys and girls at Tulane?"

Philip plopped down into a safe chair. "God, I feel like a mother hen most of the day." He tried moving his chair into the shade. "I think kids with too much money have a need to create problems. Of course, if they didn't, I guess they wouldn't need social workers, right?"

Philip had been working at Tulane for over a year, always on hand in case students needed counseling. Jerry knew that Philip loved the job, but he found it amusing to hear him bitch about it.

"Are you still a social worker when you get into that gym during the day?"

Philip stretched out his arms and flexed while looking pensive. "Well, let's see, when I'm there I'm really social, and I'm workin' it! Yeah, I guess I am a social worker in the gym!"

"You're a mess. Why don't you go get changed? I'd suggest a mint julep out on the lawn, but since it's so damn hot, you'll have to settle for a cocktail in my den."

Philip made another effort to squeeze into the shade, brushing his brown bangs off of his forehead and then wiping the sweat on his shins where his pants were already wet. "You need some more trees out here, ol' lady. It is inhumane to subject your tenants to this kind of suffering."

Jerry let out a loud 'hah'! "You wanna hear about suffering, lemme tell you–"

Philip was already out of the chair. "Oh God, spare me those old "Great Depression" and World War II stories. Okay, I'm off to shed my straight drag. I may take you up on that cockytaily, though."

Jerry grinned as he watched Philip walk away. He realized that he had a tendency to remind his young tenants a bit much about his wretched past–which wasn't all that wretched, really. But he liked to make them think it was. Looking at Philip fumble with his keys at the back door of his apartment, Jerry was almost overcome with emotion.

Such a beautiful, blessed young man. If he only knew how lucky he was to be able to work and live as a gay man without fear of persecution and harassment.

"Okay, my little chicken, the offer for the drink stands, but I may be out here for a while yet."

Philip managed to shove the water-soaked door open and extract his keys. "Alright, ol' lady, it'll take me a while for re-entry anyway. 'Re-entry.' That's a social work term, ya know." Just before he closed the door, he poked his head back out. "And don't stay out there too long. Really, you could get a stroke or somethin'."

"Yeah, right, I'm a tough old bird, remember?"

Jerry was left to himself to enjoy the quiet courtyard, interrupted occasionally by the sound of traffic coming down Burgundy Street. Other than the thrumming of tires across pavement, the soothing sound of spraying water filled the silence, almost making him feel cool, but not quite. He managed to find a bit of shade on the other side of some banana trees, and as soon as he had ensconced himself there, the gate to the back yard opened again. A smiling woman walked in.

"Hi, Jerry!"

"Well 'hi' to you too."

Jerry couldn't help but smile right back at her. Darlene was always so exuberant; she just oozed happiness.

"Dawlin', you just about the only person I know who comes home from work that happy. You on somethin'?"

She giggled, then putting her fingers to her nose, she pretended to sniff up the last remains of some coke. "Hey, I'm just happy to be here, Jer."

Darlene was probably in the urban dictionary next to the term "fag hag," even though Jerry hated that word. She was a little overweight, bright, cheerful, loving, sensitive—but a little insecure. Despite her weight, she managed to gracefully avoid the sprinkler as it dashed water around the yard. Her femininity made her so beautiful. Jerry was happy to have her as a part of his chosen family.

"You'll forgive me if I don't stop to chat, won't you?" She was digging in her enormous purse for what Jerry often referred to as "the world's largest set of keys."

"I'll live," he said, "but only if you promise to visit in about half an hour to toast the setting sun. Philip will be there."

"Great! Philip's home already?" She didn't give him time to answer that question. It was one of those responses she liked to throw out to fill space. She wasn't one to enjoy quiet, and even as she brushed back her shiny black hair with one hand and stuck her key in the door with the other, she kept on talking.

"I'd love it. It's just that if I don't get into theACsoon, my dress is gonna be stuck to me!"

Jerry watched with some amusement as she put her weight against the door to get it open. She had to shove three times before it gave way, and each time her dress hiked up a little on her hips and revealed a little more of her slip each time.

"See you in a few!" She slammed the door behind her, grabbing her skirt out of the way just in time.

Jerry sighed, knowing that he had to do something about those doors. With all the rain that had come down the previous week, the doors were still somewhat swollen and difficult to operate. His face turned to a frown. That would take a lot of energy. Another sigh as he looked around the yard.

Aw, to hell with this sprinkler. Didn't it rain enough yesterday?

"It's time for *me* to get watered," he said to himself. "Mother needs a cocktail."

* * * *

After unpacking every box except the ones stuffed with pots and pans, Barry decided to reward himself with a brief night on the town. He had followed the sound of loud music to a bar on a nearby corner, one his neighbor told him was a gay bar.

He didn't remember the bars in Dallas being this dark. Were they? Warm air occasionally drifted into the Bourbon Pub through the doors, defiantly open in the face of the September heat. Leaning against the wall near the corner, Barry found it easy to scope out the comparatively sparse weekday crowd. New faces, all. He noticed a glance or two in his direction, but then again, he was new meat in the bars here, wasn't he? He smiled to himself, feeling liberated and silently toasting himself as he raised the beer to his lips.

It was hard for him to decipher his feelings at the moment.

Am I happy?

Maybe. There was something freeing about starting over from scratch. Every now and then, as he sipped his brew, he nearly expected his recent ex, Dorian, to walk in the door, stride over with a smile, and plant a kiss on his waiting lips. Of course, this little vignette was not to be, given the fact that his ex-lover was hundreds of miles away, probably cruising some Dallas country western bar.

Barry took another swig from the bottle. Coming up with nothing more than suds, he trudged over to the bar for a second. He was keenly aware of the curious, cruisy glimpses in his direction, so he made a special effort to swagger as much as he could.

The bartender saw him coming. "Coors Light, right?"

Barry was impressed until he realized he was holding an empty Coors bottle. How difficult was that? Being in the hotel/service industry, Barry found amusing what others would find flattering.

"Yes, please," he answered, placing his empty bottle on the bar. He rested his elbows on the bar and leaned forward, taking the opportunity to get a good look at the faces he hadn't seen yet. Perfunctory glances met his gaze, even a nod from a guy at the corner of the bar. Seeing the bartender making his way toward him with a fresh bottle, Barry stood up straight, reaching into his pocket for some money.

Before the bartender could spout the price, Barry tossed some money on the bar, with a bill or two to spare. "Thanks."

"Thank you!" replied the bartender, who paused for a moment, then offered his hand.

"My name's Jeff," he said, breaking into one of those affable smiles that didn't give away too much intimacy.

"Barry. Hi."

Jeff moved a few feet over to the cash register, looked around the bar to make sure that no one was demanding his attention, then turned back to Barry. "Just visiting?"

"No, I live here." Barry blinked, and Jeff was still staring at him, acting interested and obviously expecting more, so he launched into a more verbose explanation. "I just live up the street, on Dauphine," he spoke louder, leaning in closer whenever Jeff cocked his head to the side. "I only moved in a few days ago."

"Well, welcome!" said Jeff, offering a hearty smile to his newfound tipper. "You made it here just in time for Southern Decadence."

Barry laughed. "Yeah, that was part of the plan."

Again, Jeff scanned the bar to make sure no one was left wanting. "Do you know anyone here yet?"

"No, not really," Barry answered, trying not to seem desolate. In truth, he wasn't. He could honestly say that he was not lonely.

"People here are pretty friendly." Jeff noticed a bill waving on the far side of the bar and made a perfect exit line as he turned away with a charming smile, "Somebody as good-looking as you should make friends in no time."

Barry couldn't help his natural response to the action of a man in retreat: he checked out his butt.

"He's pretty picky. You should be honored."

Barry felt caught in the act. The voice was coming from somewhere near his left elbow; he had to look downward to see that there was a woman's pretty smiling face looking up at him.

Regaining his composure, Barry bent down to her and said, "What was that?"

"I said that Jeff's pretty picky, so if he said that you're good looking, you should be honored."

"Oh, I see, so you don't think it was just for a tip, huh?"

Her giggle was unique, ending with a little squeal. "Well maybe, but still…"

"Yeah, I know: Never look a gift horse in the mouth. My name's Barry."

"Oh hi, I'm Darlene." She beamed and extended her hand, which had several rings on it. Something about her brought out the gentleman in Barry, and feeling playful, he reached for her hand, bowed, and kissed the back of it.

" 'Tis a pleasure."

This little action elicited another squeal from Darlene. "And they said that southern chivalry was dead."

Barry laughed, liking the attention. "Can I buy you a drink?"

"Why sure! I've always depended upon the kindness of strangers," she replied, with the best Blanche imitation she could muster while yelling over the music.

"Stranger is right," said Barry. "I just moved here."

"Really? Well, I should be buying you a drink! How do you like it so far?"

"Decadence was interesting. But before I tell you my life story, whaddya wanna drink?" Barry tried to get Jeff's attention.

Darlene glanced at her watch, then said, "Oh, no thanks, I'd better not. I'm just here to meet a friend before we head out to dinner."

Jeff sauntered over. "Is Darlin' Darlene gonna have a drink?"

More giggles from Darlene. "Maybe later, Jeff. I'm just here for a minute. How are ya?"

"Okay. Try to come by later, if you can. And drag Philip back with you," Jeff added, rushing toward a flurry of bill-waving.

"I'll try," she yelled after him. "I'm meeting him for dinner!"

Barry had a chance to chime in, "So maybe we can talk some other time. The offer for a drink stands."

"Thanks," beamed Darlene. "Hey, why don't you join us for dinner? My friend Philip would love to meet you."

"I wouldn't want to impose."

"Stop it," Darlene cut in. "We're just friends, and we have dinner all the time. You'll give us something new to talk about."

Barry shifted his feet, feeling somewhat uneasy. Hell, what harm was there? She seemed nice enough. It's not like she's an ax murderer or anything. Besides, he liked the company of women, more so than his ex did.

"Sure, I'd love to," he answered.

"AAH!" Darlene screamed and jumped. "Philip!!"

Laughter erupted from behind Darlene as a handsome, twenty-something man stood up straight, removing his hands from Darlene's waist.

Darlene gave him a playful slap. "God, I hate that! I'm so ticklish."

Philip moved into the circle, taking note of Barry, who was also posturing in that hey-I'm-a-helluva-man kind of way.

"Barry, this is my friend, Philip."

"Hi, Philip."

"Hey. Nice ta meetcha."

The handshake was firm, lingering just a moment longer than usual.

Darlene saw the body language and grabbed Philip's arm to jostle him from his reverie. "Do you mind if Barry joins us for dinner?"

Philip looked from her back to Barry, smiled and said in his sexiest voice, "I don't mind if Barry joins us for life."

Uh oh, thought Barry, as he grinned at the compliment.

I have a feeling I know what's on the menu tonight.

* * * *

It was now after one o'clock in the afternoon, and Joel still could not get up the nerve to walk down the hall much less walk into the office. He wasn't sure what was worse—the hell he had been living in for the past year or the hell he would live in after…after…after what? After he admitted he was…gay.

There, at least I can think the word. Maybe I can even say it.

Joel looked around his room first, then whispered, "I'm gay."

For most of his life, Joel had assumed that he was the only queer in the world. At the all-boys high school he had attended, he had heard rumors about guys, of course, but they had never been substantiated. And the way that everyone had talked about queers, Joel was convinced that he was not…one of *them*.

How could he be? He wasn't a sissy. But Joel knew one thing: He was attracted to men.

"I like guys," he said to himself, more brave this time.

There, he had professed his feelings out loud, even though no one was listening.

Coming to Tulane had taught him one thing, if nothing else, and that was the existence of other gay men. He had seen them.

During his freshman year, Joel had listened to one of the school counselors talk about "celebrating diversity." No one really knew what he was talking about, but when they heard the words "gay and lesbian," they suddenly were all ears. "Many of your fellow students here are gay," he had said, "and they expect and deserve the respect that is allotted to all of humanity."

With a wry smile, Joel recalled his observation of the rapt attention from these same guys who, in high school, probably yelled "faggot" at anybody remotely different.

"Religious and ethnic minorities are welcome here, as well," the guy continued, "as are all people. We acknowledge our diversity and find commonality in our academic pursuits…"

Joel was really impressed by the guy who gave the speech. It had been over a year since that orientation session, but Joel remembered his name and wanted to talk to him. He figured that if this guy could be so supportive of gays, then he would be understanding about his feelings.

He had made up his mind that today would be the day that he would gather up enough courage to walk to the counselor's office and talk about…IT. He couldn't wait much longer; he had a class at three o'clock.

All morning he had plotted to make the trip across campus, and all morning he had been waylaid by his fears. Suppose someone he knew saw him in the counselor's office! 'Hi, Joel. What are YOU doing here?' Or, 'Hi Joel, do you have a *problem*?' He imagined someone running across campus and telling his friend Lance, "Guess who I saw at the counselor's office! Do you think Joel is gay?"

On and on, Joel's imagination concocted horrific scenarios.

His thoughts turned once again to his terrible loneliness. What was worse—desperate fear or the terrible anguish of aloneness?

His mind made up, Joel finally left his room and headed across campus. When he was within sight of the counselors' building, he paused to look around before going any further. When he reached the building, he did a more thorough survey before going in, taking a couple of minutes to ensure that no one he knew was near the office.

He walked forward now with a purpose, his blood pumping so fast that his temples pulsed, and he could hardly hear anything except his heart's terrified thuthump, thuthump.

He walked into an office sparsely furnished with three chairs and a receptionist desk. It appeared that there was no one there.

"Can I help you?"

With a start, Joel reacted to a woman's voice that came from the far corner of the room, outside his field of vision. A woman stood there stacking some magazines on a bookshelf.

"Uh, well, no, not really."

Do I look like I need help?

"I mean, I was hoping to be able to see…"

Omigod!

His mind drew a blank. "Philip!" He had almost shouted the name like he was in a third-grade spelling bee.

"Oh, sure," she replied sweetly, walking behind her desk. "Do you have an appointment?"

Joel froze. *An appointment?* People who go to an emergency room don't need an appointment.

"Uh, no, I just thought I would drop by, and uh…well, I can see him some other time."

Joel had already begun his retreat. He could tell from the look on her face that he was acting really weird.

She probably knows. Gay guys probably act this way when they come in here. She can tell.

"Would you like to make an appointment?" She was afraid to take her eyes off him lest he bolt for the door.

"Has my two o'clock called yet?" A voice came from a hallway behind the desk, and within seconds, Philip appeared at the door.

Omigod, I've been caught naked without any appointment on.

"Sorry, I didn't know anyone was here," he said, looking at Joel.

Joel opened his mouth but nothing came out.

Sensing his discomfort, the receptionist stepped in. "Oh, your appointment called and canceled a few minutes ago. I was going to tell you when you got off the phone."

Joel's gaping had changed to a bad grin. He could feel the red in his cheeks.

"This young man wanted to drop by and…say hello. I was just going to set up an appointment…"

"Hi, I'm Philip," he said, concerned that the boy in front of him would collapse on the floor any second. He put on a warm smile and extended his hand as he walked toward Joel.

Somehow, social instinct kicked in enough for Joel to lift his hand in return, and a few words managed to find a way out of his mouth.

"Hi, you probably don't remember me. I met you last year."

Pause. Joel almost forgot to let go of his hand.

"Oh, my name's Joel," he added with a nervous laugh. He rubbed his sweaty hand on his pants just as it dawned upon him that it may have looked like he was rubbing off Philip's handshake.

"Joel, it's nice to see you again. Sorry, I meet a lot of students here."

"Oh, that's okay."

Philip did, indeed, remember this guy. A bewitching-looking creature like this was hard to forget. He reminded himself that he was at work, not play.

This kid is a wreck.

Philip knew his next step was to make Joel feel more at ease.

"Tell you what, Joel, I have some time to visit, since my appointment canceled. Why don't you come on in?"

Joel wasn't sure if he was pleased or terrified, but he managed a response.

"Sure."

Philip knew from experience that no one walks in to just "chat." This kid looked like he was on the verge of hysteria, but he also knew from experience that people like this who needed to talk only did so when they were ready.

After a few minutes of listening to Joel chat about crazy professors and classes, Philip saw that he was calming down a good bit. He let Joel rattle on, and when there was a lull in the conversation, Philip just sat, remaining quiet.

Joel froze.

"Well, it was nice seeing you again," he said in a hurry, scooting to the end of his chair. "I know you're really busy, so…"

Philip knew that he had a window here, but he knew that he had to move quickly without being overbearing.

"Joel, before you go…Do you have a minute?"

Joel sat back, looking at his watch. "Sure. I have a class at three, but that's almost an hour away."

"Well, I just wanted you to know that the reason why I'm here is to be available in case anyone just needs to talk."

Gauging his visitor's reaction and the pause that followed, Philip could tell that whatever it was that brought Joel here, it took him a lot of courage to get this far, and he knew that Joel wanted to talk about it.

I'm taking a big chance. Maybe I went too far…

"Well, if you have some time…" Joel's temples had begun to throb again. He could feel the rush of blood to his face. So much energy surged inside of him, he wasn't sure if he'd be able to remain in his chair.

Philip sat back. "I have lots of time. What did you want to talk about?"

Joel squirmed in his seat, knowing that this was the moment of truth.

"Well, you see, I…"

There was a really long pause before he could continue.

"I…"

Joel began to panic. Suppose he was all wrong about this guy? Suppose he didn't really like fags and the only reason why he said all that stuff about diversity was because he got paid to do it. Suppose…

Nearly a minute had passed, and Philip wasn't sure what was going on in this guy's head. Joel's mouth was open, he had sunk forward with his elbows on his knees, his hands wringing, his eyes bulging and glued to the floor. He looked catatonic.

Philip leaned forward. "Joel, I want you to know that whatever you say to me stays within these four walls. That's a promise."

These words seemed to have a calming effect, so Philip went on.

"I also promise that I will listen, and that it is not my place to judge. Whatever it is you have to say, I want you to know that it's okay to say it."

"I…" Joel mouthed the word "I" several times, though the sound was emitted only occasionally.

"I…I have this problem. You see, I'm g…I'm attracted to guys."

Joel blurted out these last four words so fast that Philip almost asked him to repeat them, but he knew just what was going on here, and it took every bit of will in him to keep from jumping over to comfort the poor kid.

Joel continued to stare at the floor. Philip wanted to say, "Is that all?" But of course, he didn't.

"That's okay, Joel. It's okay." Philip paused as he allowed these words of acceptance to sink in. "Everything's going to be okay."

Joel began to sob like he had never cried before.

* * * *

"Damn, this always happens," groaned Jerry, drying his hands in earnest as the phone rang for the second time. He turned the sink faucet off and grabbed the phone with the dish towel.

"Hello," he barked.

"Hey ol' lady, how about some company?"

"That depends. Who wants to visit me?"

Philip chuckled. "C'mon, you know I'm the best offer you've had today."

"The evening's young." Jerry neatly replaced the towel on the oven handle.

"The evening may be, but…"

"Watch it! Mother Landlord doesn't take well to these insults."

Philip laughed again then became a little more serious. "Really, I could use a little company right now. I just want to unwind a little with a friendly face."

"That counts me out," said Jerry, but when Philip didn't laugh at his joke, he changed his tone. "Of course, you can come over. The door's always open for you, little one."

The conversation wound down quickly, and Jerry returned the phone to its cradle.

"Let's see if I can scrape up enough food for my little lost soul of a tenant," he said to himself, rummaging through the refrigerator.

He heard a brief knock, then, "Can I come in?" As usual, Philip was already closing the door behind him without waiting for an answer.

"Damn, that was quick," said Jerry. "Yes, you *MAY* come in. You must've really wanted some company. Whatsa matter, that guy from Dallas already dump you?"

Philip walked into the kitchen, smiled and leaned on the counter. "You can't get dumped until something is there to be dumped."

Jerry closed the fridge, wielding four new potatoes and a pound of ground beef. "You mean to tell me you haven't gotten in that boy's britches yet? You younguns just don't know how to live. Youth really is wasted on the young."

"Now Jer, sex isn't everything. Maybe we want to get to know each other first."

Jerry made a face. "Excuse me! Who are you, and what have you done with the *real* Philip?"

"I know, I'm usually the one who's early to bed and later to go home, but this is different."

Jerry waltzed over to Philip in his best dramatic Florence Nightingale imitation and placed a hand on Philip's forehead. "Are you running a temperature? Maybe we should call a doctor."

"Yeah, yeah, yuck yuck yuck. Go ahead and make fun, but this time I really want to just, you know, date for a while."

Jerry didn't seem all that convinced. "Uh huh. So that's what's bothering you?"

"Oh, hell no," said Philip.

"What then?"

"Well, I'm not sure how much I can say, you know, because it involves work, but today this kid came into my office and began to cry like there was no tomorrow. It was really draining."

"What was he so upset about?"

"He came out to me. I'm not really bummed or anything. I guess I should be excited that I was able to help him at such a critical time in his life, but now I'm worried I didn't handle it right, ya know? Like I don't really know what I'm doing sometimes, and all these kids have got these problems."

"Fix yourself a drink. No, I'll fix one for you. What's your pleasure?"

"Have any ginger ale? I mean, some that's not flat?"

"My, my, we're picky today. As a matter of fact, I do, bitch."

"Okay, well sprinkle some of that into some bourbon and ice."

Jerry began puttering around the bar. Philip grew quiet and reveled in the sound of tinkling bottles in the background. He closed his eyes and thought of his mother, who made similar noises around this time of the day when he was a kid, but with pots and pans instead of liquor bottles. Coming over to Jerry's was a lot like coming home. He opened his eyes just as Jerry walked into the room with a glass filled to the brim, a cocktail napkin adorning its bottom.

"Take two of these and call me in the morning." Then he leaned in closer, leering. "Or maybe you can just roll over and wake me."

Philip sat up to receive his cocktail. "Jerry, do you always think about sex?"

"Only when you're around, darling."

Philip knew, of course, that Jerry was joking. Then again, Philip also knew that Jerry would love nothing more than to get in his pants.

"You are such a chicken hawk!"

"You're not chicken anymore, missy," Jerry shot back. He plopped down on his leather wingback, and using his right foot, pulled the hassock closer to him before propping his feet up. This little procedure of his, though simple and quick, was made more interesting by the delicate manner in which he managed to balance his cocktail without spilling a drop.

"You're too old for me now," Jerry added. He waited until he had finished his sitting-down-with-a-drink ritual before going on. "So, tell me about Barry. What's going on with him?"

"Not much to tell, I guess. I really like him, and I'm pretty sure he likes me, but remember, he just got out of a relationship that he was in for a few years. He's not overly anxious to jump into another one. But I'm not looking for a long-term commitment, either, so that's fine with me."

Jerry took a long sip. "Are you sure you're not looking for more than that?"

Philip leaned back on the couch and put his feet up on the ottoman next to Jerry's.

"Honestly, I don't know. Maybe. You know what a romantic sap I am, deep down, even though most people think of me as being shallow."

Jerry's face melded to sincerity.

"Darlin', people who know you don't think that. But with those pretty brown eyes and that shiny brown hair, you just flirt your way around town. That's probably what people think—that you're a flirt."

Jerry paused, and Philip looked up to smile at him. He knew Jerry wasn't finished, just taking a break to light up a cigarette.

"Godammit I hate these things! Childproof, my ass. Adult-proof, more like it."

"Gimme that!" Philip grabbed the lighter from Jerry's hand. "I may even join you. You know, just to be polite."

Jerry chuckled. "I guess that means you want to bum one."

Philip pretended to be offended. "Do I look like a bum or something?"

"No, but you look an awful lot like my tenant Philip, and *he's* a bum."

Philip laughed as Jerry tossed the pack at him. He fished out a cigarette for himself and lit them both up—Jerry's cigarette first, of course.

Jerry drew long and hard, then took a swig from his drink.

"Where were we? Oh yeah, we were talking about your-"

Jerry stopped mid-sentence when Philip stood up and began to walk away. "Uh…NOW where are you going?"

"Just to get more ice! Don't fret, Mother, I'm coming right back."

"Well, hurry up, dammit."

Jerry sat back and waited, the sound of a rattling ice tray in the background.

That boy is always so antsy.

"Okay, I'm back. Madame was saying?"

"Uh, that's 'Mademoiselle.' I was saying that you're a flirt—and there's nothing wrong with that—but you should let people see the other sides of your personality."

"Hmph." Philip mulled it over. "Most guys want to see my other PARTS, not my other sides. Know what I mean?"

Jerry snickered. "Yes, I know what you mean, but I don't get many such requests anymore."

"Speaking of wanting to see parts, I asked Barry to come with me to that fundraiser next week."

"Great! What fundraiser? Am I invited?"

"Jerry, you're more than welcome, but I promise you, it's gonna be a drag. It's at that horrible old Charlie Tilton's house."

"Oh my GOD!" Jerry exclaimed. "Is he still alive?"

"C'mon. He's not that old."

"I know. But I thought by now someone would have killed him." Jerry shuddered. "You're right, I don't want to go, but tell Barry I send my love."

Philip sunk into the sofa and took a gulp of his drink. "I can't figure out how to send Barry MY love, much less anyone else's."

* * * *

Linda tugged hard at the steering wheel, trying like hell to fit into a parking spot on a skinny uptown street.

"How much room do I have?" she asked for the second time.

Dottie opened the backseat window and peered out. "You're about a foot from the curb. And I think you have about a foot between you and the Saab."

"Screw it," Linda mumbled. She crept in reverse until she felt a slight bump, at which point the Saab's alarm went off.

"Linda!" Patricia screamed, covering her ears with her hands. "I'm so embarrassed!"

Linda inched forward, hitting a BMW in front of her. It, too, began to wail.

"Christ, people shouldn't buy these cars unless they can afford a driveway." Linda backed up a tad and shut off the car. "Quick, let's get out of here before we attract a crowd."

The three of them leapt from Linda's slightly used Honda, which looked even more "used" when framed by the two European models. Their destination was over a block away, and they could see a few guests near the front door, craning to get a look at the commotion. A bevy of gay clones began to meander their way, pushing their alarm buttons and glowering at them.

Giggling like high school girls, the three crossed the street to avoid the accusatory glances of the oncoming clones. When they arrived at the house, the alarms had subsided, but they were still the objects of curious scrutiny as they approached the door.

"Wait!" huffed Patricia.

"What's the matter?" asked Linda.

"With all that commotion, I didn't have a chance to check my makeup."

Dottie rolled her eyes and looked over at Linda, who had a similar exasperated look.

"C'mon, Patricia, you know you look just fine. Believe me, if there are any other dykes here—which I doubt—you will look more than lovely in comparison."

"Hmph," said Patricia, opening up a compact mirror she had grabbed from Linda, who always carried a purse. "It's not the dykes I was worried about. It's these vicious uptown queens."

With that ritual completed, they strode up to the front door, making their way through a crowd of ten or so guys who were amicably chatting, cocktails in hand.

Patricia approached the one nearest the door. "Excuse me, do you know where we might find Charles?"

The man turned to her, somewhat surprised at having been addressed by a woman. "Uh, not really, but I last saw him in the kitchen, giving the help a hard time."

Patricia smiled, knowing full well that he was serious. She really wasn't into this whole crowd, but her wealthy parents had made sure that she always knew the right people. Charles Tilton was one of the right people. Of course, he was perhaps the most pretentious man she knew. She sighed. Were it not for the fact that this was a fundraiser, she wouldn't be caught dead here, even though Charles was renowned for his parties.

Seated at a table in the foyer was a man about twenty years old and handsome, as were all the young men who worked at Charles' parties.

He smiled at them, revealing, as she expected, a perfect set of white teeth.

"Good afternoon, ladies. Do you have your invitations?"

"Sure," answered Patricia. She was naturally expected to handle these situations, since she was more accustomed to hanging out with this crowd.

The three of them wandered into the living room, where Linda and Dottie gaped at the lavish furnishings.

A man's voice came from behind her. "Well, thank God we finally have some women at this thing."

Linda turned to see a familiar face. "Oh, hi Sky!" She gave him a hug.

"Just to be politically correct, we have to make sure there are at least a couple of token women at these high society events." Sky cleared his throat dramatically. "We wouldn't want people to think we're gay or anything."

Dottie snorted. "Do any of these men even know any women?"

"Sure," said Linda. "They clean their houses."

"C'mon, y'all, it's not that bad," said Sky. He looked around at the crowd, then turned back to them with a grin. "Well, maybe it is."

Patricia scanned the room along with the others. Dottie and Linda seemed considerably more out of place, crossing their arms and rocking back and forth on their heels.

Trying to start some conversation, Patricia turned to Sky. "So how's that horrible business you have?"

"About as horrible as yours," he answered, and they gave each other a knowing smile. Both of them owned galleries on Magazine Street. Sky had an antique shop, and Patricia had a small art gallery, where she displayed her own work.

"Oh, Steven sends his regards. He might show up later. Wait…Where are my manners? I haven't even given these other two beautiful women a kiss yet."

Dottie and Patricia pretended to be love-stricken and lunged at Sky, each of them taking a separate cheek to kiss. This charade caused a bit of a stir, so there was a momentary stillness around them as people glanced their way.

"Oh God," whispered Dottie, looking around, "I think we may have broken some Uptown rule of etiquette. By the way, where's Philip? He was supposed to be here."

"I already talked to him," said Sky. "He's here with a Tulane students as well as that green-eyed beauty from Dallas he's been dating. Knowing Philip, all you have to do is look for the spot where the largest crowd is gathered, and he's probably right there in the middle of it."

Patricia's brow furrowed with curiosity as she asked, "What was that about being here with a student? Is it someone he counsels at Tulane?"

"I don't know," answered Sky, "Maybe. You know how careful he is about divulging information," he added with a smile. "He's an adorable kid, probably a freshman or sophomore. I have a feeling that this party may be his first gay event ever."

"Oh my God," said Linda, "I don't know if being with all these snotty queens is such a good introduction to the gay scene."

"There we go again," said Patricia, "We're always joking around about these people, but they're not that bad. Think about it. At least they care enough to come to a charity. They could be off…I don't know, shopping or doing coke or something."

"Okay, you have a point there," said Linda. "It's just the attitude some of these guys have."

"Overall, I think it's a good event for a first impression," said Dottie. "Don't you think it would be worse if he just went to a bar like everybody else?"

"That's true," chimed in Sky. "But bars aren't necessarily bad places. It's just that some people take advantage of…you know, people new to the scene."

Patricia leaned over and asked, "You mean virgins?"

"I heard 'virgins.' Is anybody talking about me?" The host, Charles Tilton, waltzed over with his left hand palm up, shoulder height, and his right hand daintily holding a cracker covered with brie.

Everybody gave a slightly embarrassed laugh, and in turn greeted their host.

"We were on our way to say hello to you, but got sidetracked," said Patricia.

"And you, my little Sky. Aren't you lovely!" Charles' hand came down just long enough for him to tweak Sky's cheek. "I could just eat you like this Brie!" He took a little nibble on his cracker and looked around. "Oh, isn't this crowd just faaaabulous!" Charles lifted his hand a little higher and gestured toward the crowd, his dyed hair so black it reflected light from the chandelier above. A gorgeous man of about twenty-five passed just then.

Charles threw back the rest of his cracker and exclaimed, "Oh, my dearies, I feel like I've died and gone to heaven!"

Dottie and Linda exchanged glances, grimacing to control their laughter.

Patricia reprimanded Linda with an elbow to the ribs. "We were just saying that this would be a nice place to meet people."

"But of course, deary," Charles proclaimed. "Everybody who's anybody comes to my parties. Well, mingle, girls. Mingle!"

Charles left in a flurry of cashmere and lace, his left hand back in its perpetual palm up position.

"He is too much," said Dottie, as she and Linda released their pent-up laughter.

"He is pretty funny," said Sky. "I guess when you're that rich you can act as silly as you want."

"Okay, you can have fun now. I'm here!" It was Philip, making his way through the crowd.

The three women gave Philip hugs while Sky stood by, staring at…what? Philip was obviously getting ready to launch into a story when Sky loudly cleared his throat.

Everyone turned toward Sky, who gestured with his chin toward a young man standing just behind Philip.

Philip said with a start, "I'm sorry, Joel!"

He grabbed Joel by the elbow and pulled him into the circle.

"This is Joel, a student from Tulane. These are my friends Linda, Patricia and Dottie. You already met Sky, right?"

Joel had an ashen look about him as he said "hello" to the group, then a stunning silence followed as everyone stared at this newcomer, who looked overwhelmed—or downright terrified—by his first experience of a group of gay people.

Linda broke the silence. "What's your major, Joel?"

"Huh?" Joel had begun to look wide-eyed at the men surrounding him when Linda's question jolted him back to reality. "Oh, um, business."

"Do you like it here?" Patricia asked.

"Yeah, everybody here seems to be pretty nice," he answered, looking around timidly.

The others in the group exchanged smiles, and Sky chuckled softly, one of those nostrils laughs.

"Joel, I think what she meant was, do you like it here in New Orleans? You're not from here, are you?"

"Oh! I'm sorry." Joel laughed nervously. "I thought you meant…you know. Um…yeah! I like it. And you're right, I'm not from here. I was reared in Ohio."

Charles appeared out of nowhere.

"What was that? Ohio? Oh, sugar, then it's time for you to be reared in New Orleans, isn't it?" He squealed and reached over with both hands to grab the sides of Joel's face, then squeezed his cheeks before leaving as quickly as he had arrived, this time with both hands in the air.

No one moved, not quite sure how to continue a conversation after that kind of exchange. Joel's mouth stood open, and his pale face turned beet red just as he began to tremble.

Oh God, thought Philip, he's probably thinking that he'd rather be straight right about now.

I guess we'll be having more than one counseling session this week.

A hunk squeezed into their circle, saying to Philip, "I thought you had abandoned me."

"Not quite, just too quick for you," answered Philip. "Does everybody know Barry? Good."

Before anyone could answer, Philip grabbed Barry and Joel by the arm. "I think we've had enough. I mean, we have to get out of here…I…uh…we'll see y'all later."

Philip was already halfway to the door, pushing Barry ahead of him and half-shielding, half-dragging Joel behind him.

Charles tried to cut them off at the door, but the three of them bolted. Sky and the three women watched the hilarious tableau come to an end and then looked at each other in disbelief, uncertain if they should be amused or concerned. Patricia broke the silence.

"I told you this would be an interesting party. Drinks, anyone?"

* * * *

Joel turned up the volume to the stereo, losing himself in the sweet sounds of Anita Baker.

"…You'd better watch your step. You'll fall and hurt yourself one day…"

He returned to his lounge chair, where he had been ensconced for most of the day. He was still trying to recuperate from his first experience with other gay people. He stared into space, watching the tiny particles of dust reflecting the light that streamed in from the window.

It was a bright sunny day outside, and Joel had thrown open the curtains, hoping that the sun would lighten his mood. Instead, he only felt all the more melancholy, his temperament bleak and in stark contrast to the world around him, which was alive and crisp with autumn.

The door opened, and in stepped Lance.

"Are you going deaf or something?" Lance asked, walking over to the stereo to turn it down a notch.

Joel didn't move an inch, feeling rooted to the chair. Lance seemed like nothing more than an imaginary being, made more so by the way that the light seemed to radiate from his blond hair and white tee shirt. The dust particles swirled as Lance swam through them as he moved across the room, lending more credence to the illusion of Lance as a golden-haired angel.

Lance made sure that the volume and settings were just right on his stereo, with which he was somewhat obsessed. He turned around to look at Joel, and was somewhat taken aback by his somber appearance.

Joel's eyes moved to take in the image of Lance, still framed in a halo of light. Lance had to squint to see Joel, since the light was in his eyes.

"What the hell's the matter with you?" he asked, leaning over and playfully slapping Joel on the thigh. Lance was smiling as he performed this gesture, but as he leaned over into the shade where Joel was sitting, he was stunned to see a tear winding its way down Joel's cheek.

Lance froze, then slowly lowered himself to the floor at Joel's feet, his face a mixture of open concern and surprise. "Oh, man. What are you crying for? Did something happen?"

Boy, DID something happen! I was just humiliated by a bunch of queers!

Honestly, Joel hadn't realized that he was crying. His entire life he had wept interior tears. He thought the pain he was feeling now was the same and then cursed himself for lowering his defenses.

The silence in the room was deafening, despite the soulful voice of Anita in the background.

"…It's so easy to tease me. It's so easy to let me down. It's so easy to mislead me. It's so easy to leave me hanging around…"

Lance stayed in his position, vigilant at Joel's feet and utterly concerned for his friend's welfare.

"C'mon, man, you're really beginning to scare me. What's wrong?"

Joel was a little frightened by his vulnerability. He had been discovered to be the sappy sentimentalist that he was, and he didn't want Lance to see any more. But despite his efforts to control his emotions, he quickly surrendered to the overwhelming feelings as they washed over him in waves of loneliness and despair.

The first tears didn't flow easily. At first his body began to quiver, as though he were warding off some demon from within. Perhaps he was.

The sobs started from his gut. Joel covered his face with his hands and leaned over, elbows on his knees. Then the tears came in torrents. Lance placed his hand on Joel's shoulder, lightly rubbing his fingers back and forth from the tip of his shoulder to his neck. This affection was very comforting, but it only made him cry all the more when he realized how much he had been longing for human touch.

There was another reason that made Lance's touch all the more meaningful. For over a year now, Joel had longed for just such a touch from Lance, and now he found himself crying a little longer, maybe just to keep physical contact with the man he wanted to love.

Then, try as he might, Joel simply could not cry any longer. He was spent. He felt the mixture of relief and exhaustion that comes from vomiting after an upset stomach.

And I haven't even started vomiting yet. I wonder if he'll still want to be touching me when I tell him I'm a fag.

Joel straightened up a bit and wiped his face with his hands. Lance reached over to the nightstand for a box of tissue, then resumed his position on the floor.

"Here you are, man." Lance gave him the entire box. "Are you okay?"

Joel ripped out a couple of tissues before placing the box on the floor. He didn't know what to answer. "I don't know, Lance. I really don't know."

He really didn't know. The counselor had assured him that he was okay, but he hadn't yet accepted the idea.

"Then what's going on?" asked Lance, a bit more insistent this time. He got up and sat on the edge of the bed, as close to the chair as he could get.

Joel was surprised by Lance's compassion. He never really perceived Lance as a caring, sensitive kind of guy. Yet here he was, consoling him, unaware of what Joel was about to tell him.

Joel wanted so badly to simply blurt it out, but the fear of rejection swallowed him whole and left him in its belly.

Lance simply sat there, patiently waiting.

Joel still didn't know what to say, but he was afraid the silence might deafen him.

"Lance, we're really good friends, right?"

Lance winced. It was subtle, but Joel sensed it. "That's a stupid question, man. You're my best friend."

Lance had never called him his "best friend" before. Joel was moved.

He asked, his voice quavering, "So whatever I told you, we'd still be friends?"

"Of course!" Lance sounded injured. "You know that's a silly question." He leaned over and placed his hand once again on Joel's leg.

Joel blurted out, "What if I told you that I was gay?"

Joel could feel an immediate tension in Lance's arm, suddenly frozen on his leg. He tried to imagine what was running through Lance's mind at that moment. Perhaps he was thinking things like, 'Do I remove my hand now? If I do, am I rejecting him? If I leave it, is he going to think that I'm a fag, too?'

That moment may have only been a few seconds or less, but for both of them, it was an eternity.

Joel continued looking down, afraid to see what was in Lance's eyes. His heart sank when he felt Lance remove his hand from his leg. His flustered coming-out to Lance had broken through a dam of pent-up isolation, but the feeling of liberation was fleeting. Now there was a cold spot, burning, where Lance's hand had been. Joel resigned himself to fear's darkness as he closed his eyes and placed his hands over them, prepared to fight back the tears that might come. But now the old defenses began to rise, and he told himself he could cry no more.

But when next he felt Lance's cheek next to his, Lance's hands warm on his back, Lance's tee shirt collar near his nose and his breath on his neck, Joel melted into him.

"I'd still be your friend," said Lance, pulling Joel closer and rubbing his back. "And you'd still be *my* friend. My best friend."

Joel discovered that he could, indeed, cry some more.

* * * *

DaShawn

It was quiet for a Sunday at Lazarus House. DaShawn was surprised that there weren't more visitors. He raised the straw from the glass of water to the resident's lips. He took a few sips then lay his head back on the pillow.

"Thank you." He looked up with gratitude into DaShawn's face.

"You're very welcome, Roy." DaShawn smiled back at him and put the glass of water down next to the bed. He noted that Roy had lost weight since his last visit. His pale cheeks were starting to get that hollow look that he associated with HIV.

"Is there anything else I can get you?"

Roy struggled to focus. "What's your name again?"

DaShawn's heart broke a little, but he managed a gentle smile. "It's me, DaShawn. You know who I am."

Roy's lip began to tremble, and DaShawn's heart broke a little more. He fought to control his emotions.

I can't cry. I can't cry. Be strong!

He sat down on the edge of the bed. "Do you mind if I sit for a while?"

Roy's lips turned into a smile. "I'd love that."

DaShawn reached for his hand and Roy's smile grew even more.

"You know," said Roy, "I dated a black guy once."

DaShawn tittered, surprised. "Is that a fact? Well, it wasn't me, was it?"

For a moment, Roy frowned, but when he looked up into DaShawn's grinning face, he knew he was joking.

"I'm not one of those white guys who thinks that all black men look alike."

DaShawn laughed again. "Well, that's good to know."

There was a gentle knock on the door. "Okay if I come in? Sounds like a lot of laughing going on in here."

DaShawn looked up to see a familiar face. "Hey, Philip! Come on in. Roy and I were just having a little chat."

Philip walked around the bed and grabbed Roy's other hand. "Hi, Roy. It's nice to see you."

Roy was feeble, but you could see his eyes dancing as he glanced from one to the other.

"This reminds me of the good ol' days," he smiled. "Tag-teamed by two hot guys."

The "two hot guys" laughed.

"I've never had that happen to me," said Philip, then he leaned closer to Roy and grinned. "Not yet, anyway."

DaShawn chuckled. "Hey Roy, do you mind if I borrow this guy for a minute? There's something I need to discuss with him."

Roy nodded, looking much more cheerful than he did a few minutes earlier.

When they were out in the hallway, Philip whispered, "What's up? You need to talk privately?"

"Nah, this is okay. I just wanted to say hi. How are things at Tulane?"

"Same ole. Every student's crisis is the world's worst. Things okay with you?"

DaShawn frowned. "I guess so. Still working with addicts. It's not what I had in mind when I got my MSW, but it's a job. I wish I could do more HIV-related stuff. I mean, I like volunteering, but I want to do more."

Philip could sense that DaShawn needed a morale boost. "Hey, let's get together soon. We can form a support group over cocktails. How about tea dance today?"

DaShawn stepped back and gave him a puzzled look.

"You still go to tea?"

Philip looked down, a little embarrassed. "Not often. Just every now and then. Come to think of it, since I've been dating, I'm not even sure when the last time was. We can do something else. It was just the first thing that came to mind."

"It's been a while for me," said DaShawn. "I think the last time I went was on my twenty-fifth birthday. I walked in, looked around, and I felt so OLD."

Philip giggled. "I know the feeling. I'm a little older than you, remember? So thanks for nothing."

"Hey, we're not even in our prime yet!" DaShawn insisted.

"We're not exactly chickens, either. Okay, then meet us at The Mint on Friday. I want you to meet my future ex-husband."

They heard Roy fall into a coughing fit, so they rushed back into the room to find him holding a half-empty glass and still spilling water.

"You okay, Roy?" DaShawn took the glass from his hand while Philip began to dab the water from his chest.

Roy's coughs subsided. "I'm okay. Just went down the wrong pipe." He fell back into his pillow and closed his eyes. The coughing fit had exhausted him.

DaShawn brushed Roy's hair back off his forehead. "I'll be back to check on you in a little while."

"See you later, Roy," said Philip, giving his shoulder a goodbye squeeze. Then he pointed at DaShawn. "And you I'll see Friday. Don't forget!"

A moment later, as DaShawn began to move away, he was surprised when Roy grabbed him by the wrist. He was a bit unnerved by the intensity of Roy's gaze.

"Quite a firm grip you got there, Roy." DaShawn smiled. "Can I get you something?"

Roy's brow was furrowed in concentration as he gazed at DaShawn, then his expression lightened, morphing into a wistful look. "You know, I dated a black guy once."

DaShawn chuckled. "Is that so?"

* * * *

Lance was in a panic.

Joel is GAY?

As Joel cried on his shoulder, Lance's mind was a maelstrom of feelings and thoughts spinning and crashing against each other. Then his inner turmoil was subdued by a gentle stream of powerful memories—good memories of the times he and Joel spent together, the many times they had laughed, the hours they wiled away lounging on the sofa watching TV, the things they had done, places they had seen…

Lance began to calm down a little.

Joel is the best friend I have ever had.

He didn't realize that until now. He recalled the times Joel had helped him with algebra and English comp—the times when they had sat close together at the desk, when Joel reached across him to point out an equation, the way he looked in that ripped tee shirt he refused to throw away, how his lips moved, his smile, the curve of his jaw, the way his hair smelled right after taking a shower, the feel of the muscles in his arm brushing against him, his smooth skin touching him…

Are his lips on my neck?

Lance began to panic again.

* * * *

The Pub had a nice crowd tonight. It was a little too chilly for the doors to be open, though there were men wandering in and out of the bar, restless.

"D'ya ever notice how some men just can't sit still in a bar? How they have to keep moving around?" Philip directed this question at Barry, who sat languidly at the small table they were sharing.

"Philip, I can't believe you have the nerve to ask that." Barry put down his drink and glanced toward the doors, checking out the men coming in. "You can hardly sit still for more than a minute."

"Who, *moi?*" Philip leaned back in his chair, feigning innocence.

Barry smiled. Philip's antics were always entertaining. He was a lot like his old boyfriend, but Philip was definitely more mature.

The last few months had been quite a challenge for Barry. He had moved to New Orleans from Dallas with a sense of hope and purpose, symbolically and literally cutting himself off from his past. He had visited New Orleans before, of course, since Dallas wasn't all that far away, but New Orleans had a strange, captivating charm about it that was magical. Moving to New Orleans was Barry's way of jumping into the future without a care in the world.

"Are you even listening to me?" asked Philip.

"What?"

"I didn't think so. I was saying that we should make some plans for the new year."

"Whaddya mean?" Barry was surprised by the question, and now he realized that he had probably sounded defensive.

Philip's face registered understanding, then broke into a smile.

"Oh, for crying out loud, Barry, I'm not asking you to make plans with me for ALL of next year. God knows how afraid you are to be stuck with one man again. All I'm asking is to make plans for Tuesday night…you know, the thing we call New Year's? New Year's Eve?"

"Oh. I knew that."

Barry hadn't known that, and Philip was right. He was scared of getting too involved with one man, even though he couldn't imagine a much better catch than Philip.

But he and Philip had met during his first week in New Orleans, before he really had a chance to go out and enjoy being single again.

"Man, you are eerily distracted tonight." Philip reached across the table to grab Barry's hand, which he squeezed tightly then quickly let go. Philip didn't even want simple gestures like hand holding to be construed by Barry as some attempt to tie him down.

"I'm sorry Philip. I would like to talk more candidly about what's on my mind, but I don't really think a bar is a good place."

To make his point, just then a more than slightly tipsy man jostled his chair, nearly spilling the drink in his hand.

Philip broke into one of his toothy smiles then leaned over raising his eyebrows up and down, suggestively. "Well, why don't we take it over to your place, where you can slip into something more comfortable. And then slip out of it."

Barry tried for a second to be serious, but soon he was smiling, as well.

"Philip, you have such a unique way of putting things. Okay, let's go."

Ten minutes later, the two of them were sitting on Barry's couch in his apartment on St. Philip Street. Barry was sitting sideways and Philip was nearly horizontal, with his feet in Barry's lap.

"Okay, we can talk about whatever you want to, but only if you rub my feet while you're doing it.

Barry pretended to be disgusted. He made a face and turned his head to the side, simulating breathing difficulty.

Philip shoved his toe into Barry ribs. "Cut it out! You're the one with stinky feet, not me. And you and I both know what a foot fetish you have. I can already see you're getting hard."

Barry lifted up Philip's feet and looked down toward his crotch, acting surprised when he noticed a slight rise there. "Nah, it looks like that ALL the time."

"Yeah, you wish!" Philip tickled him in the ribs some more. "Okay, so what's going on? Did you really have something to talk about or was this simply some cheap trick to get me into your lair?"

Barry remained quiet, staring into the distance, searching for the right words.

As Philip observed him, he was overcome by Barry's presence, his beauty. As he looked over at Barry, the first thing he noticed, as always, was his green eyes, which screamed like a beacon in the night. But it was more than that. There was a sadness about Barry. He was a gentle warrior who had been wounded in battle and didn't quite have the fight he used to. Notwithstanding that, there was something about Barry that always made him feel safe, protected. When he was with Barry, he felt like he was with a security guard—no, it was more intimate than that— he was with his guardian angel.

"Have I ever told you that you have a striking resemblance to my guardian angel?"

"Are you going to let me talk? Or are you going to just ramble all night long?" Barry asked.

56

Philip was still in the mood to play around, but his perceiving side told him that it was time to listen.

"Okay," he said, removing his feet from Barry's lap and curling them up underneath him. "I'm all yours. What's up?"

Barry removed his shoes and assumed the same pose as Philip on the other end of the sofa.

There was a moment of intense silence interrupted only by the sound of their breathing and the noise made by their jeans rubbing lightly against their bodies as they settled down. Then, just silence. And they both felt it setting the mood, like a blanket covering them, like meditation, the passage into another mode of being.

When Barry's words came, they were halting. "I need to be upfront with you, Philip."

The silence took over again, and time crawled as they both held their breath—one trying to think of what he was going to say and the other anticipating the worst.

"What I mean is…I think we may be moving a little too fast for me."

Barry looked up at Philip, whose face was beginning to drain of color. He could practically hear Philip's heart pounding, the pulse in his neck a giveaway that he was upset.

"Now, don't get upset, Philip. I want us to keep dating. Really, I do. And I don't really want to date anyone else. But I want a little more time for myself. A little more freedom."

Philip was taking it all in. This was no real surprise for him. He thought it was only poetic justice, since he was always the one to put the brakes on. He took in a deep breath, crossed his arms, tilted his head back and looked at the ceiling.

After a few moments of silence, he looked back at Barry and smiled.

"Okay, Barry. I understand. And that's okay with me."

Barry relaxed. "Great. I knew you'd understand."

Philip stretched his legs out once again, replacing them in Barry's lap.

"Of course, I understand." He broke into that toothy smile and again moved his eyebrows up and down, suggestively. "Well, now that the talking part is over, why don't we slip into something more comfortable?"

Barry grinned and began removing Philip's socks. "Why don't we just get naked?"

* * * *

"Okay, David, Daddy's dry." Jerry raised his empty glass as proof. The ice cubes had not finished melting, but the vodka was decidedly absent.

David appeared within seconds with a fresh cocktail and a new napkin, which he plopped down in proper order.

"Boy, that was fast," said Jerry, surrendering his former glass. He gestured with bravado. "Take this away!"

The bartender laughed as he took the glass.

"Are you okay, Jerry?"

David had been counting, and he knew that Jerry was probably pretty close to the limit. He wasn't all that concerned, because Jerry lived only two blocks away and wasn't going to be driving home.

In answer to David's question, Jerry raised his eyebrows without raising his head, which didn't seem to be cooperating with his wishes, anyway.

"I'm fine, hon. Ju…ju…just enjoying my retirement."

David smiled and walked away.

A couple of Jerry's companions sat to his right, their eyes glued to the television, trying to play that damn trivia game. He thought about the fact that he really didn't prefer the company of people his own age, retired and in their sixties. He felt a lot more comfortable with younger people, especially Philip, his tenant.

"David, are you sure Philip didn't call here?" he asked, his words slightly slurred and his eyes beginning to open and close slowly.

David moved back over to Jerry's corner, "No, dear, for the hundredth time, Philip didn't call. You know how he is. He's probably solving the life problems of some Tulane brat."

"He'll show up," insisted Jerry, leaning with both elbows on the bar. Even with this extra support, Jerry realized that he was having difficulty maintaining his balance. His body swayed back and forth, the front of his oversized polo rubbing against the edge of the bar.

He felt like he was about to slip off of the barstool, so, using his left hand to grip the bar firmly, he stood up a little, adjusted his warmup pants, and squarely plopped back down on the stool.

"Rush Limbaugh!"

The yell startled Jerry.

"Yes, I think you're right," said another.

"You scared the crap outta me," slurred Jerry. "What was the damn question?"

"Who uses the term 'feminazi?'"

Jerry went to take another sip of his drink, but when his hand missed the glass the first AND second time he tried to pick it up, a little alarm went off in his head. A very faint alarm, dulled as his senses were, but an alarm nonetheless. He motioned for David.

"David, honey, d'ya mind getting me a waterback please? I think I need to thin out my blood a little."

Jerry said these words slowly, carefully—so slowly, in fact, that by the time he finished the sentence, there was already a glass of water in front of him.

"That's probably not a bad idea, Jer," said David, picking up the nearest ashtray and expertly dumping the butts in the nearest trash can.

More yelling to his right and across the bar—"What? Who has a guitar shaped like a what?"

"A hieroglyphic. Or was that hieroglyph…"

"Prince!"

"No! The symbol formerly known as Prince."

"What the hell is his wife's name, anyway? Mrs. Symbol?"

A round of guffaws.

"The former Princess?"

Hawhawhaw.

Jerry started feeling down, really down. He imagined that he could feel his blood, the cells themselves inebriated and confused, looking for a place to go.

"Even my body's confused," he said.

"What was that?"

"Oh, nothing, just talking to myself."

Jerry closed his eyes and saw the blackness, spotted with green lights surrounding a whirlpool of red. He felt himself being pulled into the red swirl, falling, falling…then his head drooped, knocked over his water, and nearly hit the bar.

"Looks like I got here in the nick of time," said Philip, who had just walked in. He put an arm around Jerry, then with his other hand he lifted Jerry's chin to get a better look at his face.

"Jerry, you're a mess! Hey, Darlene! I'm over here."

Philip motioned to Darlene, who had just walked in and was peering into the bar, her eyes adjusting to the dim interior. At the sound of Philip's voice, she acknowledged his call, nodding and making her way to the bar, squeezing between the stools and the wall. She was short, but she wasn't exactly small.

"Hi, Jer!" she said with a smile, her friendly face lit up, as usual, in a perpetual state of contentedness. "What's goin' on?"

Jerry grunted in response.

"Oh, Jerry here was getting ready to take a nap at the bar, is all," said Philip. "You mind givin' me a hand here?"

"He's a lot of man for me to handle," she said, "but I'll give it a try."

"Thass right," Jerry slurred, "I am a (hiccup) a lot of man."

"Lord," said Philip. "C'mon, Jerry. Let's go."

As soon as the cold night air whipping down St. Ann Street hit Jerry's skin, he felt a sudden burst of energy and alertness.

"Okay, kids!" he said with a smile, faltering between them as they gently led him around the corner of Dauphine Street. "This is great! Just like old times! Where are we going now? The Roundup?"

Darlene squealed with delight. "That's a great idea, Philip. Let's go!"

Still holding one side of Jerry's swaying body, Philip leaned forward and admonished Darlene.

"Don't egg him on. Are you crazy? The only place we're going is home."

Jerry stopped suddenly, causing the two others to stop as well, nearly pulling Jerry down to the banquette.

"What are you stopping for?" asked Philip.

Jerry shook free of them for a second, pushing his elbows outward in a show of pride and independence. He didn't seem to be falling, so Philip and Darlene let go but stayed warily close to him.

"I need to get a few words in…here." Jerry raised a hand to wipe his face then cleared his throat as if preparing for a grand speech.

"You're my friends, and I...I...you're my...friends," he said. He closed his eyes and raised his arms.

"Come give your ol' landlady a hug."

Philip managed a smile, tossing aside his concern for the moment. Darlene and he moved into Jerry's arms, and they shared a group hug, which was cut short by the fact that Jerry was perilously close to falling again.

Darlene giggled, spilling musical laughter as she helped Philip steady their doddering friend and landlord.

Philip's face had returned to a concerned frown, but a gentle smile was underneath it. "We love you, too, you ol' fart, but I'll love you more tomorrow."

Jerry began walking with them again as they dragged him across the street at the corner of Orleans.

"Oh! You'll love me, will you? But will you re...respect me in the morning?'

Philip laughed and said, "Oh yeah, Jer, but I have a feeling you may not respect yourself with this hangover tomorrow."

"Oh, don't you worry about Mother, hon. Mother's gonna be fine."

They walked along quietly for a moment, the sounds of Darlene's heels echoing in the chasm between the walls that lined Orleans Avenue.

Jerry's head was beginning to clear, making room for nostalgia and sentiment. He thought of the blessings of his life and closed his eyes for a moment to thank God for his friends. Then he smiled, knowing that he was with two of his favorite people in the world.

"Okay, home we go," said Jerry ...as if they were taking him any place else. "But I have one favor to ask."

"Oh Lord," moaned Philip, "here it comes, Darlene."

"How...how 'bout a night cap?'"

* * * *

"C'mon, Lance, I can't believe I'm the one who's actually begging you to get out and do something." Joel was eager to spend some time with Lance, just the two of them. He had been pleading for some time, but Lance wasn't answering.

Usually the calm, collected type, Lance was fidgeting with the stereo, nervously shifting from one foot to the other, avoiding eye contact with Joel. He took a deep breath, then quickly exhaled, drawing himself up as he did so.

"Look, Joel, I have to say something."

Joel gazed steadily at Lance, who resumed his uneasy shifting. The silence in the room grew. When he realized that he had been stalling for close to a minute, Lance turned and looked Joel in the eyes. He averted his gaze to the floor.

"Joel, you and I have been friends…since we were freshmen, right?"

Joel's reply was cautious. "Um…Yeah."

Joel felt a strong sense of dread. He knew him well enough to know that whatever Lance wanted to say was going to be something that he did not want to hear.

When Lance still didn't answer, he repeated his answer. "Yes, we have. So?"

Lance moved closer to the door, and for a moment Joel thought that he was going to bolt from the room. Instead, he stopped at the desk, leaned the back of his legs against it and folded his arms across his chest.

God, he looks sexy, thought Joel. He tried not to be obvious as he glanced at Lance's forearms, lightly covered with smooth blond hair, the taut muscles under his skin twitching every time he moved. Joel knew that this was the way he acted when he was tense about something.

Around everyone else, Lance exuded confidence, never flinching under any type of social duress. Everybody thought of Lance as the hot 'n' hunky man on campus who "had his shit together," but Joel knew better. Since they had become roommates, Joel had seen Lance at his worst. Sometimes it was a broken heart, or more often, Joel was there to pick up the pieces after Lance's chats with his father, who was a demanding tyrant.

Right now, Lance was acting a whole lot like he did after one of those phone calls from his dad. Joel already knew what Lance was getting at, but his heart just didn't want to deal with it.

Lance made another attempt to start a sentence, only to hang his head in confusion. Or was it conflict?

Joel was getting antsy just sitting there, so he blurted out, somewhat angrily, "Lance, just say it! What is it?"

Lance jerked his head up, surprised at the tone of Joel's voice, looking a little hurt at being addressed so crossly.

His eyebrows arched, like he had made a decision to launch forward, whatever the cost.

"Joel, I'm…" His voice didn't come out as confident as he had intended, so he started over again. "…I'm afraid that you may have gotten the wrong idea."

Joel felt his chest tighten as a wave of pain moved up through his chest and into his neck. His mouth went dry, and his tremulous swallow had nothing to carry with it. He cleared his throat and spoke carefully.

"What are you talking about, Lance?"

Lance looked cornered once again, ill-prepared for any question from Joel.

"Joel, you know, the other day…when you told me you were, uh, gay?"

Joel's reply was terse. "Yeah?"

Lance looked down at his feet. "I think I may have given you the wrong impression."

The dryness in Joel's throat turned to a huge knot. He stared and numbly blinked.

Lance jumped straight up and said, "I'll be right back. I, uh, wanna get something to drink. You wanna Coke or something?"

Joel was afraid he wouldn't be coming back. "Sure, Diet Coke. Thanks."

Lance turned the knob and went out.

"Lance!" Joel fairly yelled.

Lance stopped short, poking his head back in the door with a frightened look.

"Do you need change?" Joel asked.

"Oh, no, I got it." Then Lance was gone.

Joel leaned back in his chair, trying to shake his anxiety. He closed his eyes and thought back over the recent events that had changed his life so much. He wanted to relive that moment, a week earlier, when he had told Lance he was gay…

When Lance had proven to be so receptive to his coming out, Joel had sobbed in his arms. When he had felt Lance's cheek next to his, his hands on his back, and his breath on his neck, it seemed natural to respond.

Without forethought, after a minute or so of sobbing in Lance's arms, Joel began to nuzzle Lance's neck with his lips as he was crying. Lance didn't seem to mind, so Joel put his arms all the way around Lance's body. Still no negative response, but Joel did notice one thing: Lance's heart had started to race, matching the pounding of his own.

Joel slowly moved his head so that it rested on Lance's chest, and as he looked down, he was surprised at what he saw there, throbbing and growing with each passing second. Joel had held back his feelings for so long, and he was afraid that this opportunity would never come again.

A flood of loneliness, frustration, and longing combined to give him the courage to lift up his head and kiss Lance squarely on the lips. And Lance, uneasy and slow to respond at first, soon met Joel's kiss with resounding passion, grabbing Joel behind the head and forcing his tongue into Joel's mouth.

Joel was afire with longing, wanting to give himself over to Lance—his friend, the man for whom he had longed since he had first met him. Finally, he could be with someone he loved. Finally, he could experience what he had wanted all along.

It hadn't occurred to him before that Lance could possibly reciprocate his affection, but there Lance was: on top of him, on the floor; holding him, kissing him.

As Joel was reliving those moments, a smile had crept across his face, and he had to adjust himself. Just the memories made him excited. He closed his eyes again…

He wasn't sure what to do next, but he knew he wanted to do it, whatever IT was. He moved his hands down Lance's back until they rested on his butt, which he squeezed.

Like lightning, Lance hurriedly stood up, and without saying a word, he pulled his shirt out of his pants to cover up his erection, and he ran from the room…

The past few days had been hell. Joel wanted so badly to revisit the intimacy of those few minutes, but Lance never acknowledged that anything had happened, and he was always finding some reason to avoid spending time with Joel.

Now, for the first time, Lance was talking. And he was denying it all.

The door opened and closed, and Lance strode in and handed a soft drink to Joel.

"Thanks, man," Joel said, popping open the top.

"No problem." Lance returned to his position leaning against the desk.

Joel was still worked up from his reminiscence, and he was feeling brave, as well as a bit horny. He took a long sip, for courage, then stared directly at his roommate.

"Lance are you going to try to deny that you had feelings for me when we were kissing the other day?"

Lances eyes seemed to bulge from his head, and he went white with anxiety.

"We weren't really…kissing. I mean…"

Joel couldn't help but smile to himself. Here was this gorgeous hunk of muscles before him, nearly blubbering with fear. It made him desire him all the more.

Joel stood up, going with his gut.

He walked across the room, and Lance looked like he was going to pass out.

"Yes, Lance, we were. Like this."

Joel kissed him lightly on the lips, and Lance pulled back.

"I don't…"

"Shh," Joel whispered. "It's okay." He leaned over to fill the space between them, and once again his lips met Lance's. This time, Lance didn't pull back. He began to quiver. He moved his hands up to push Joel away, but when they touched his chest, they simply stayed there. Then they found Joel's back. And pulled him closer.

* * * *

It was after midnight when Philip opened his window and looked out onto the patio behind his apartment. The crisp winter air gushed in, immediately giving him goose pimples. Cold though it was, he leaned out of the window to take in a few deep breaths. The traffic on Burgundy Street was steady, but not too heavy this late at night. He looked around the patio, noting the dead vegetation that had not survived a couple of light freezes this winter season.

He smiled to himself as an image of a frustrated Jerry came to his mind. Jerry worked all summer long to keep the courtyard lush and beautiful, only to be annoyed year after year by one single overnight freeze that left the patches of ground brown and looking defeated.

Philip's smile faded. He closed his eyes.

What's the difference between that grass and my own life?

Every year he met someone that he thought was Mr. Right. Every year he worked, pruned, watered the relationship, and every year, the frost came.

The thought unnerved him.

He opened his eyes, reached out to close the shutters, then forcibly pulled down on the window, fighting the sash, until it closed with a firm *fump*!

This was always a difficult time of the night for Philip. Just before bedtime, he always got lonely, longing for someone to curl up with him in bed. Long, chilly nights were even more difficult for him, especially in a drafty old apartment like this one.

He shuffled across the floor, his white socks collecting a little dust as he made his way to the thermostat in the living room.

No, he was wrong, the floor furnace was turned up high enough…he walked over to it…yes, it was on. Why was he so cold?

"I know why I'm cold," he said out loud, laughing almost bitterly. "Because I'm always expecting warmth from someone else."

He stood over the floor furnace for a while, enjoying the heat as it moved up in waves, lifting his nightshirt gently, and letting it fall back again. The hair on his arms and legs vibrated from the warmth as he soaked it in. He stood there until the hair on the back of his neck began to stand up and the heat began to seep through his thermal socks to his skin. He moved quickly then, with a humorous "ow" escaping his lips as he jumped off of the grate.

"I'm getting burned by everybody and everything today."

He plopped down on the sofa, propped his feet up on the coffee table and stared at the slow spin of the ceiling fan overhead.

He knew that he was probably overreacting. Barry had gone away for the weekend to visit some friends back in Dallas, and Philip was feeling abandoned. He and Barry had been dating for about three months now, and this was only the second weekend that Barry had not been in town. The other trip had also been to Dallas, because Barry had left a few personal items there, after his split with his ex, and he decided that he would go back for the weekend to sort through some items in storage, so that they could divvy up those shared items.

Philip didn't really have any feelings back then. That was over two months ago, and he wasn't all that attached to Barry at the time. This weekend, he had to admit, he was feeling a little jealous. He tried not to, but he kept imagining Barry back in bed with his ex, Dorian, holding him against his chest, making plans to reconcile their differences and move back in together.

Philip shook it off, quickly leaning forward to grab the remote. Maybe he could just watch the boob tube for a while…just long enough to put him to sleep on a Friday night. Home alone.

The sound came on first. CNN.

"Oh God, that's all I need. More reality."

He hastened to change the channel before the video caught up with the audio with some frightening image of a war-torn neighborhood SOMEWHERE.

"I don't think I can stand the sight of Sally Struthers tonight. I'm going bonkers already," he said.

HBO. John Travolta.

"This is about as close to un-reality as I can probably get."

He had already seen this movie twice, but something about John Travolta and Christian Slater duking it out in a box car amused him, so he declined the urge to surf…for the time being.

Was that a knock on his front shutters? Nah, probably the TV was too loud. It seemed to coincide with Slater slamming against a wooden crate.

Knock. Knock. Knock. A little louder.

Philip was instantly on guard. He swung his feet onto the floor, fumbling for the Mute button. He found it, then listened for a few seconds. "Who is it?"

"Philip, it's me, Joel."

Shit, thought, Philip, what the hell is he doing here?

"Uh, hang on a minute, Joel, okay? I've gotta find my keys."

Philip's keys were right by the door, and he knew it, but he was trying to buy some time to slip out of his nelly night shirt and into something that a counselee would expect a counselor to wear at night.

Like what? A suit and tie?

Philip grinned at the absurdity of his concern.

Screw it! This is my house, and this is the way that I dress before going to bed. He'll have to deal with it.

"I'm coming."

Philip found the right key, opened the door, and then unlocked the front shutter. As he pushed on the shutters, he saw Joel backing down the steps to let him swing them open. Philip wasn't really quite sure if he wanted to let Joel in, so he said, "What's going on? Are you okay?"

Joel started to answer, but he was taking in Philip's appearance. He knew Philip as the social worker at school—preppy, definitely good-looking, but almost dorky in a professional kind of way. Here he was in a flannel nightshirt, the muscles above his knees flexing and showing a good deal of tone.

His calves are pretty nice too...

Joel looked up at him and smiled, recovering. "Nice outfit, dude."

Philip wanted to say something really sarcastic, but this was, after all, a client. Kind of.

He had been seeing Joel for two or three months now, trying to help Joel deal with coming out. Through the process, Joel had discovered that Philip was gay, too, which complicated the situation a bit, since it was not uncommon for clients to fall in love with their therapists. Or, in this case, with their social workers.

"Yeah, yeah, I'm a regular model, right? Is there a particular reason why you would bang on my door after midnight?"

Philip was trying to be professional, but the truth of the matter was he was glad to have some company, even if it was one of his students from Tulane.

The smile fell from Joel's face. "Oh. Your light was on, and..."

His first attempt at an explanation faded away.

"Well, I'm really sorry, Philip. Really, I am. But I think I'm going crazy. You said that if I ever needed to talk..." He let the sentence hang there, not knowing how to finish.

"You're right, Joel, though I think I meant at my office. Do you want to make an appointment for later this weekend? We can..."

"Oh, Philip, I'm sorry, I really am, but I have got to talk to someone tonight."

Philip weighed his options. It would be far from appropriate for him to let a client into his house, unless the situation were dire…and Joel didn't really look like he was in a crisis. Another danger was the fact that, even though Joel was just a student, he was only a few years younger, and he was also incredibly beautiful.

"Philip…" Joel said.

"Huh?"

"Um, I know that this is an…an odd situation, but could we please talk about this inside?" Joel was looking toward the corner, where a man was walking along in the shadows in their direction.

"Sorry, Joel. C'mon in."

Philip moved to the side, his hand still on the shutter. "Hurry up. It's not always safe this time of night."

Joel walked up the stairs and brushed against Philip as he passed him, squeezing into the cottage's narrow doorway. He could feel it. It was a little like the feeling he had when he was with Lance, but different. It was a kind of electricity that passed between them.

Philip felt it, as well, and quickly reminded himself that he was a professional and that he could not act upon such urges.

"Something to drink?" Philip asked.

Joel looked up at him, surprised. "A drink?"

Philip smiled. "I meant water, or a soft drink. Not a cocktail."

"Oh. No thanks."

They sat down, Philip in a chair and Joel on the couch.

"Did you come down here just to see me?" Philip asked, trying to uncover the motives behind this strange visit.

"Oh, no. I was at The Parade."

Hmmm, thought Philip, *Is this the same guy that hated gay men last week?* Time passed. The silence would prod Joel eventually, he knew.

Joel looked at his feet for some time, then grinned and looked up at Philip. "Well, I'm not a virgin anymore."

Oh brother, thought Philip. "What do you mean?"

"Lance and I are in love! I've decided that he's the man I want to be with for the rest of my life."

Lord, give me strength.

Philip wasn't sure he'd be able to handle this crazy naiveté this late.

"I see. Well, do you mind if *I* have a drink?"

Philip got up, but he didn't walk to the kitchen; he walked toward the liquor cabinet. He wouldn't need ice for this drink.

* * * *

Linda was staring again. She looked away and cursed herself for being so obvious. She couldn't help it. There were so many little things about Patricia that she found alluring—the way she walked, the way she tucked a stray hair behind her ear, the way her eyes danced when she laughed. And that thing she was doing right at that moment, nibbling on her lower lip while she was painting.

They had plans to have an early afternoon picnic at the Lakefront, but when Linda called Patricia to say she was on her way over to pick her up at her studio on Magazine Street, Patricia said she needed a little more time to finish up some work first. Linda gave herself permission to look at her again.

She is so irresistible when she is painting...

Once again, thought Linda, here I am waiting on Patricia. It bothered her that it didn't bother her. She was usually annoyed by people who were always late, but not when it came to this woman. She believed it might be possible for her to just sit and look at Patricia for hours at a time. She was pretty sure she had never felt this way before. She wasn't exactly a kid, but the butterflies in her stomach made her feel like a teenager.

"I don't want to interrupt you, but could you at least give me a timeframe? Like, closer to five minutes or fifty?"

Patricia looked at her, wide-eyed, like she'd been in a trance.

"Huh? Oh, I'm sorry, Lin." She turned back to her canvas. "I'm almost at a breaking point, because I would need to mix some paint soon."

Linda smirked. "And that 'breaking point' might occur when?"

Patricia had already gone back into a trance. "Huh?" She didn't even turn to look at Linda. She just kept dapping at the canvas while she mumbled.

"Oh, less than five minutes, I promise."

Linda let out a loud sigh—so loud that it may have broken the spell. She was looking at the side of Patricia's face, but she could just make out a corner of her mouth turning into a smile.

"I kind of hate to stop painting," she said. "Since you got here, I have been painting like a fiend."

She stepped back, eyeing first her work, then her girlfriend. "You're my muse."

* * * *

A few days had passed since Joel's late-night visit, and Philip had squeezed in a couple of late-afternoon appointments to help Joel through this critical stage. It was already after five o'clock when Philip arrived home, but the sun was still high enough to cast light into the yard behind the old cottage on Burgundy Street. Jerry and Darlene were there, chatting side by side in two lawn chairs that they had pulled into the pool of light remaining in the yard, its shimmer ebbing with the setting sun.

Though it was still winter, a recent warming trend gave them respite from the previous week's chilly snap.

"Trying to get a tan already?" Philip asked.

Jerry and Darlene turned to look at Philip, surprised and obviously happy to see him.

"It's never too early to tan," said Darlene. "Besides, I've got a lot more to tan." She lifted her shirt to show what was undoubtedly an ample belly.

Philip smiled as he ambled over. Darlene was as tall as she was wide, but her heart was biggest.

Jerry reached over to lay his hand on her belly, as though he were feeling for a pulse or a kick.

Darlene shrieked and pulled her blouse back down. "Your hands are freezing!"

"Oh, sorry, that was my cocktail hand." Jerry shifted his drink from one hand to the other to prove his point, the glass half empty but filled with enough ice to make a gay tinkling noise as it traveled.

"I might as well join you," Philip said. The two moved over a bit to make room for him as Jerry pointed to a lawn chair a few feet away.

"Oh, I don't want to tan," he laughed. "I meant that I'd be glad to join you for a drink. This is perfect weather for something light and refreshing."

Jerry swirled the dirty vodka around the inner rim of his glass and tilted his head dramatically in Darlene's direction.

"He must be talking about us," he said to Darlene, grabbing his chest with his free hand. "We're so light and refreshing."

Darlene giggled, "I can believe the refreshing part, but I don't think that I've ever been called 'light'."

Jerry removed his hand from his chest and playfully slapped at her, casting aside her put-down.

Darlene didn't perceive her comment as a put-down, because she wasn't bothered by her size. She was fat. So what? People always seemed to be overly conscious about her weight, but she was happy just the way she was.

She shielded her eyes with one hand, squinting to see Philip. He and Jerry were chatting about plans for the back yard.

"I'm having a Pimm's Cup," she interrupted. "You want one?"

"That sounds great," said Philip. "I can make it, I think. I just don't have the stuff to do it. You, Jerry?"

Jerry squinted up at Philip. "Would you puh-*lease* stand over here away from that wall? It's blinding me!"

Philip smiled, sashaying as he moved to the other side of their chairs.

"That's not the sun, Jerry. That's my radiant beauty."

Philip put a hand behind his head and pranced, his hips wagging. Because he was so well-built, his performance was especially comical.

"I don't know how that beefy boy Barry can put up with all that nelly," said Jerry. "Just tell him to call me if he needs a real man."

Darlene fumbled around beneath her chair, coming up with a pitcher and another cup. "I thought you might be coming, hon, so I made a little extra. I guess you'd call it a 'Pimm's Pitcher' instead of a 'Cup'."

Philip gratefully reached for the go-cup. "I'll just call it a 'Delicious Darlene'."

Darlene's face changed, as if she had just remembered something shocking.

"Speaking of real men," she said, "I heard someone in your apartment last weekend while Barry was out of town."

Jerry was instantly alert, and his eyes focused on Philip with unwavering judgment.

"I knew it! The cat goes away for the first time, and you're out with the other mice! I knew it!"

Philip looked a little hurt. "C'mon, y'all. It's not what you think."

"Oh, Philip," said Jerry, feigning disgust. "And Barry was such a nice man."

Philip started to say something, but he was stymied by his friends' conclusions.

"I can't believe y'all," he said, genuine sorrow in his voice. "Nothing happened. He was just a student."

Jerry and Darlene exchanged glances of puzzlement.

Darlene was skeptical. "A student at midnight?"

Jerry's head snapped back in Philip's direction. "Midnight??!? Was that how late it was? What were you doing with a student that late?"

Philip had to admit that his reputation with men wasn't the best in the world. But since he had become a social worker the year before, after having attained his MSW at Tulane, he had been meticulous about separating his personal life from his professional life. He was always very strict about behavior and ethics.

"Y'all have got to listen for a minute. Please!"

Darlene and Jerry pretended to be upset, but they were masking smiles underneath a thin, scowling visage. They were enjoying this show with Philip on the hot seat, since he was usually the one to poke fun.

Philip began to tell them the story of his weekend, about his loneliness due to Barry's absence, his unexpected visitor who regaled him with tales of his new love, and so on.

"Why did you even let him in?" asked Jerry, who was unusually quiet during Philip's recounting of the details.

Philip sat on the edge of the lawn chair and took a big gulp. "Like I'm going to leave someone on the sidewalk in this city late at night. He wasn't there all that long."

"Well, IT doesn't TAKE that long," said Jerry, breaking into laughter.

Philip lightened up a little when he realized his friends weren't really all that concerned. He sat back and smiled, putting his hands behind his head as he did so.

"With Barry, I take as long as I want."

"Oh, for Pete's sake," said Jerry, while Darlene howled.

"Well, Philip, honey, since I introduced you two, I'm assuming that one day I'll be the maid of honor?"

Philip took another swig and said, "Sorry, I already promised Jerry that role. Well, matron of honor, anyway…"

"Bitch," Jerry spat.

"…But speaking of that…"

There was a pause as Philip beamed and his two friends waited for more.

Philip cleared his throat. "Would you like to kiss the bride-to-be?"

* * * *

Barry was scared, and he admitted it. He had lived in New Orleans less than a year, and he was going to move in with someone he knew for less than a year.

Less than a year! What if I'm making a big mistake?

It was Monday night at the Bourbon Pub, and Barry was having a beer and watching some of the funny videos. Usually, they made him crack a smile, and with Barry, that was pretty hard. Tonight, nothing seemed to be able to pull him out of the funk that he was in.

He took a swig from his bottle and glanced around the room. Wow, he thought, these faces are beginning to look a little too familiar. Less than a year ago, when he had first moved to New Orleans, he was the new kid on the block, but now, he thought, I'm nothing more than tired old meat on the butcher block.

He groaned quietly as he took another sip. There was something a lot different this time around, though. When he lived in Dallas, he had spent a few tumultuous years sleeping around with men who worshipped him for his looks. Finally, he had settled down with Dorian, but only after he had been on the bar circuit for a while. He lived with Dorian for a few years before they decided that the relationship was over.

He moved to New Orleans, thinking maybe he could recapture those earlier days of wild abandon, when nothing seemed to matter but the music of the night: the games that happen after dark and in the wee hours, when men become lost spirits groping in an underworld of illusion and fantasy.

Barry pulled a stool closer to the table and sat down, leaning his arms heavily on the oval table, upon which he placed his sweaty bottle. He stared down at the table, thinking about his life.

Things just weren't what they used to be. He wasn't twenty-five anymore. He was in his mid-thirties, and sex and excitement weren't necessarily in the same equation anymore.

What he wanted was…something new and different. Yes that was it, he needed something like a breath of fresh air. This thought popped into his mind as a sultry breeze wafted into the bar from the door which was slightly ajar, inches from where he was sitting. He turned his nose into the warm breeze, delighted with the early signs of spring and summer.

Fresh air, that's what he needed. That's when he thought of Philip. Yes, Philip. He thought of Philip's laugh, so musical it lifted Barry's spirits from their depths; his smile, that told Barry that everything was going to be okay; his brown eyes, which in Philip's case were windows to the soul, where he sometimes saw the pain of a squandered past—a life full of "frantic tumbles and shy good-byes," a life that was behind him. But what he saw in Philip's eyes, most of all, was love.

Love. That's what scared him. But it was also the reason why he decided they could move in together.

Barry looked back down at the table, somewhat surprised that he had removed all of the paper from the bottle and shredded it up in into a pile in the middle of the table.

How embarrassing, he thought, looking around. He often criticized people who possessed such neurotic little habits, and here he was doing it himself.

Maybe I'm getting fucked up.

The bottle was nearly empty, but he wasn't sure he should get another one. It was only his first beer, but he had come straight to the Pub from the hotel without having supper. In fact, he realized that he had not had anything to eat at all since the late breakfast that he grabbed at La Madeleine on the way in to work. His mind drifted back to Philip.

Dammit!

Barry had promised himself that he was going to go slow this time. He didn't want any connections. He didn't want to be tied down. This time, he wanted to shop around and find someone that was just right for him. Someone like…Philip.

Barry heaved a great sigh and made his way over to the bar. What the hell, he thought, trying to catch Jeff's attention. He did the usual scanning of the bar while he waited for his drink, noticing a couple of new faces.

They looked his way, the ancient game of posturing in full swing.

Jeff didn't seem to want any idle chat tonight, so Barry threw a tip on the bar and walked back to his table, sitting in such a way that he could keep an eye on the cuties at the bar. He noticed that one of them was adjusting his own seat so that he could, in turn, keep an eye on Barry.

Not bad, thought Barry, taking a long look from the corner of his eye, while the other fellow looked away.

Barry couldn't help but think of this game as similar to the little routine that dogs went through when they met one another. There's the usual butt sniffing, but sometimes, one dog will pretend that he doesn't notice that the other one is sniffing his butt. He couldn't help but chuckle at the thought of gay men sniffing each other's butts.

Barry felt his mood lifting. Maybe this second beer was what he needed to make him relax enough to enjoy himself. Then again, getting cruised usually managed to lift his spirits a bit.

He looked over at the guy again. He was of medium height, but with nice, wide shoulders and a compact body that looked like he was in shape, but not with that phony, pumped-up look.

He hadn't seen him here before, so Barry guessed that he was probably visiting. But something about him…

The man's eyes locked with his. Barry smiled. The stranger looked suddenly petrified. No, he's genuinely shy, thought Barry. That realization was accompanied by another. Barry looked closer, then told himself that the guy couldn't be more than twenty years old.

"Shit," Barry whispered to himself. Another smile crept onto his face when he realized the age difference.

Hell, at least I can still attract them.

He started cruising the guy again. This time the stranger seemed more willing to flirt, seeming to warm up to Barry's signals.

Suddenly, Barry closed his eyes and shook his head.

SHIT! What am I doing?

He had spent the last few days thinking about Philip and the possibility of a long-term relationship, and here he was again, cruising someone fifteen years his junior.

The fear swept over him again. He thought of Philip and their conversation the week before…

"I know it's scary, Barry, but we spend every night together anyway, right? Moving in may not be a bad idea, especially since we could save a lot on expenses…"

Barry took a really deep drink from his beer this time, remembering his decision…

"Okay, Philip, let's do it."

With those words, he realized, he had perhaps sealed his fate. Another swig.

Maybe I can just fool around with this guy a little, he thought. Would that hurt? The justifications began to line up, one after the other.

Uh oh, Barry thought, as he noticed the guy stand up and walk in his direction. There's something familiar about him…

"Hi," said the young man, reaching out his youthful arm to clasp Barry's hand in his own. His brown eyes smiled in sync with his lips.

There was something familiar, but…

"You're certainly the most beautiful thing on two legs in here tonight," said Barry, trying his best to hypnotize his prey with his steely green eyes. The beer seemed to revive his predatory techniques. But his compliment seemed to make the kid more nervous.

"Uh, thanks," he said, shifting from one foot to the other, glancing at the floor then back at Barry. "You don't remember me, do you?"

Uh oh, thought Barry.

The boy leaned a little closer.

"I'm Joel, one of Philip's students."

* * * *

Jerry was still a bit sore at Philip.

"You almost gave me a heart attack with that 'bride to be' comment."

Philip reached over and patted Jerry's hand. "I thought it would make it easier for me to tell you that I'd asked Barry to move in. I was afraid you'd get mad. You know how you are."

"What does that mean?"

Philip laughed. "Jerry, you *know* what I mean! How many times in the past week have you told me that the water bill was going to skyrocket?"

"Oh, that." Jerry paused. "But it will go up! And there's more wear and tear on an apartment when there are two people living in it."

"Yes, you've mentioned that a few times as well, and that's what I wanted to talk to you about."

Jerry's eyes widened. "You're not going to move, are you?"

Philip raised an eyebrow. "Why do you ask? Afraid you'll miss me?"

"I didn't say that! So you're giving notice?"

Philip could see that Jerry was on the verge of distress, so he decided to stop playing with him.

"No, Jerry, stop worrying. I'm not going to move. What would I do without you?"

Relieved, Jerry reverted to his salty self. "You'd have to start buying your own cigarettes, I guess."

Philip laughed. "And my grocery bill would go up!"

"So what do you need to talk about?"

"Well, Barry and I talked about it, and we are going to pay you an additional fifty dollars a month after he moves in."

"You're going up on your own rent? That's a first for me."

"Besides, you never have raised my rent, and I've been here over three years."

Jerry quipped, "Maybe I should go up even more."

"Hush," Philip chided him. "You know you won't, and you also know that you're thrilled we're offering some extra money."

"Maybe." Jerry smiled. "Thank you, precious. I graciously accept."

"Good! That's settled then. Starting next month. Let's seal the deal with a cigarette, shall we?"

"I'm guessing you didn't bring your own," said Jerry, already handing a cigarette over.

"Oh, you're so good to me, Jerry." Philip pretended to be emotional.

"Yes, I am. Glad you noticed. And for the record, little one, yes, I would've missed you."

* * * *

"No, not there," said Philip, gesturing wildly at Barry, who was carrying a box into the kitchen.

"Put in over here, on the floor," he continued. "If it's on the counter I won't be able to see what kind of crap—I mean stuff—you have in there."

Barry bent over and groaned as the box of pans hit the floor with a clatter. "Very funny. I guess everything you have is priceless, right?"

Philip gave him an affectionate kiss on the cheek.

"Of course, honey. Like George Carlin says, 'Everybody else's stuff is shit, and my shit is stuff.'"

Barry made his way back to the door. "Well get ready, because there's more 'shit' outside."

Philip watched Barry go out, noticing the line of sweat that ran down the middle of his shirt.

Everything about him is so sexy.

He surveyed the "damage" to his apartment. He knew Barry's moving in was going to be costly to his orderly home. Fortunately, Barry was a minimalist, so he didn't have a whole lot of stuff.

"But he has enough 'shit,'" Philip mumbled to himself.

He kneeled to see what was in the latest box that Barry had deposited.

"What about this one?" asked Barry, returning with a smaller box.

"What's in it?" asked Philip, madly scanning the room for a free spot. There weren't many left in his one bedroom apartment.

"This is the last of the kitchen stuff," Barry said. "A few cups and glasses, I think."

"That's easy," said Philip. "Store it. I…*we* have enough of those already."

Barry gave him a blank look.

"What's wrong?" asked Philip.

"Store it? Where?" Barry implored, incredulously. "On the roof?"

Philip got up from the floor and walked over to Barry, not able to keep his hands off him.

"I've got something I need to store," said Philip, grabbing Barry from the back and giving a strong pelvic thrust.

"Cut it out," said Barry, good-naturedly. "I'm the one who does the storing and packing around here, remember?"

"As a matter of fact, I don't remember." They smiled at each other, sharing a grab and a kiss.

They still hadn't had the "big sex," and they were always joking about who was going to be first to do…it.

"I'll ask Jerry if he has some room in that storage shed in the back," said Philip, going to the back door. "If it's just cups and glasses, that should store well."

Barry put the box on a small corner of the kitchen counter. This time it was his turn to take a look round.

"Wow," he muttered. "This place looked small before; now it looks tiny."

Barry went over to the sink to get himself a glass of water.

"Can I come in?" came a voice at the back door.

Barry turned to see a familiar round face on the other side of the screen. "Sure Darlene, it's more your home than mine, I guess," said Barry, going over to give her a kiss as she pulled the screen door behind her.

"How's it going? I saw the back door open and figured I should take a peek."

Barry sighed, following her glance around the crowded room. "There's not enough space in here for two grown men."

"That shouldn't be a problem, then," giggled Darlene. "Philip's not a grown man yet."

"That's what it is! I knew it!" Barry hollered. "That makes me a pedophile, I guess."

"You need some help?" Darlene started shoving boxes away from the middle of the room, peeking as she went. "I hope you don't mind, but I'm a little on the nosy side."

Barry made his way back to the front door. "We have nothing to hide. Nothing from *you*, that is."

It was a bright, sunny day, and even though it was only early April, the signs of summer were all around. The heat rose from the banquette and blacktop as he crossed the street to his car.

He was lucky that he had found a legal parking spot right across the street from the house. That wasn't going to happen that often in this part of the Quarter, he reminded himself.

He opened the trunk and looked inside. There were two boxes, and only two or three more left at his old apartment. These boxes were small enough that he was able to stack them on top of each other to make it inside in one trip. Even with his hands holding two heavy boxes, he felt a weight lift off of his shoulders, realizing that the burden of moving was almost over.

As he went up the front steps, he heard loud voices inside. He walked in to find Jerry hollering at Philip and Darlene.

"Look at this! I don't have room for all of this stuff in my shed! What do you think this is, a storage facility?"

Philip scowled and waved his hand dismissively toward Jerry. "Come off it, Jerry. We only need to store a couple of boxes, not all of these. And you know damned good and well that you have plenty of space in that shed. What do you have in there, anyway?"

"My gardening equipment, for starters, and…"

Darlene and Philip cried out in unison, "GARDENING?!??"

Jerry looked hurt. "I have tools in there!"

Darlene laughed. "Jerry, all you have in there is a hosepipe and a shovel, and you know it."

"That's not true! I think there's a rake and a hoe in there, too!"

Philip laughed. "You're the only 'ho' that goes in there!"

"Ha, ha, very funny." Jerry was regaining his humor. "All right, you've made your point, but just leave me a little space in the middle to move around, okay? I don't want to trip over boxes when I go in there."

Barry jumped in. "We'll be neat. I promise."

"Oh hi, hon." Philip beamed. "Welcome home!"

"Not sure if we are going to be welcome very long if you keep abusing the landlord like that."

Jerry clapped his hands in glee. "Thank you, Barry. YOU are welcome to stay. There is plenty of room for you. But you should know that Philip will make it seem awfully crowded in here."

"Jerry, you're so histrionic," said Philip. "What are you going to do when Barry and I have kids?"

"That's not even funny," said Jerry. "Anyway, who'd be the daddy?"

"We'd be two mommies," said Philip. "We're feminists, remember? Besides, we're going to adopt Joel. I'm afraid that's the only way I can keep Barry from flirting with him."

Darlene gasped, "I heard about that! Barry, shame on you! Flirting with one of Philip's students."

Barry winced at the memory. "Look, I'm embarrassed enough, okay? I feel like a chicken hawk."

Philip gave Barry a serious look. "You are, darling. I'm barely legal, remember?"

Barry made a face and Philip lunged at him, throwing his arms around his neck.

Barry pretended to push him away. "You wish! You might be a little younger than me, but honey, that odometer of yours has quite a few miles on it."

Philip said tenderly, "Wanna trade me in for a newer model?"

Barry brushed his lips against Philip's. "Nah, I finally got this one broken in."

"Oh, for Pete's sake," said Jerry, heading for the door.

Darlene followed. "Wait for me, Jer. It's getting a little hot in here."

"You're right," he said, holding open the screen door for her. "Let's let the lovebirds make their nest."

"C'mon," said Philip, his eyes dancing with mischief as he focused on the man before him. "I've started a nest in the next room."

* * * *

The shrill sound of an alarm clock came from across the room. Philip and Barry lay motionless. They were both wide awake, but both of them were trying to ignore the damn thing, hoping that the other would make the first move to turn it off. As usual, Barry lost in the game of possum, and he slowly pushed himself up to a sitting position; but he wasn't about to admit complete failure. As he swung his legs over the side of the bed, he threw a punch in the general direction of Philip, who was still and quiet as a mouse on the other side of the bed.

"Ow!" said Philip, pretending that he had been rudely awakened for no reason. "What was that for?"

Barry walked across the room and reached for the snooze button before answering.

"Don't even pretend that you don't know why I did that, or I'll do it again!" he said, playfully.

Philip smiled back through sleepy eyes, yawning and raising his arms out from under the covers and over his head in a huge morning stretch.

"Coffee ready yet?" His question was barely intelligible, as the yawn subsided into a drowsy slur.

Barry tried to glare at him, but he found it difficult to even pretend that he was angry with Philip, who was so deceivingly innocent-looking as he sprawled under the sheets, one leg carelessly thrown over the side of the bed, exposing just enough thigh to move Barry's mind to other thoughts.

Barry's glare turned to a gleam. "Have time for a quickie?"

Philip's eyelids flew open once again, but his gaze remained narrow, as though his eyes had a mind of their own, trying to decide if they wanted to let in more light and face the day. They slowly widened as he pondered Barry's proposal.

"Well, if you have to think about it, I guess I don't want to do it, either!" Barry said, walking back over to the bed.

Philip's eyes followed his movements across the room. He smiled, saying, "I guess it depends on how good that coffee is."

Barry stood over the bed and over Philip with his arms crossed, acting displeased.

"I'm not into bartering. You either want it or you don't."

Philip pulled his stray leg back into the bed and rolled onto his side, closer to where Barry was standing.

"Don't you think I'm worth at least a cup of coffee?" he asked, reaching out to caress Barry's leg underneath his robe.

Barry mulled over that question, then he slowly began to nod his head sideways.

Philip gasped and yanked on a handful of Barry's leg hair.

"Ow!" laughed Barry. "I was just kidding. I guess I'd better make some coffee before you get really violent."

Philip rolled back to the middle of the bed. "That's right, buddy. I'll hurt you if you don't spoil me the way I deserve to be spoiled."

He watched Barry as he walked out of the room and into the kitchen—not a very long walk, since it was adjacent to the bedroom. He closed his eyes and pulled the sheets up under his chin, enjoying the last moments of rest before he'd have to make a break for the shower.

The morning ritual was becoming routine: Barry would get up and make some coffee, then jump into the shower. Philip would groan and mumble until Barry served him coffee in bed; then they'd sit in bed for a few minutes before Philip would jump in the shower while Barry dressed, and then Philip would throw on his clothes, etc.

This morning was a little different, because it was Friday. There was always an added excitement on Friday mornings, because there was only one work-day between them and the weekend.

Philip discovered that he was smiling, so contented was he at this moment. His mind went immediately to the man in the kitchen, who had miraculously become such an important part of his life in such a short amount of time. Philip had never been in a long-term relationship before, and even though he and Barry had not made any long-term plans, Philip had to admit that he was hooked. He was in love with Barry.

He never realized how happy he could be with someone. He thought of the many men that he had dated in the past six years. He was nineteen years old when he came out while he was still a student at Tulane, and almost immediately he had begun to date as many people as he possibly could.

Maybe too many, he thought, opening his eyes and staring at the ceiling.

Philip had gained a reputation for being somewhat flighty—not in the sense of being air-headed, but because he could be so non-committal. That's why he thought his relationship with Barry was so intriguing.

Barry had been in a relationship for a few years, and when he met Philip, he had only been single for a few months. Barry was definitely the marrying type, and he obviously wanted to settle down, but in this case, Barry was the one who was reluctant to make commitments and not Philip, because Barry didn't want to jump into anything too fast, and he had told Philip as much.

Barry rushed back into the room. "If Your Highness can wait, I'll take a quick shower and serve you as soon as I get out."

Philip stuck out his tongue at Barry as he walked into the bathroom.

Barry yelled from the bathroom, over the sound of running water, "That's why I like you so much. You're so mature for your age."

"Don't talk about age, old man," retorted Philip, who promptly threw a pillow at the bathroom door, causing it to slam shut.

He heard Barry chuckle on the other side.

It seemed that no sooner had the shower turned on that it was off again and Barry was out of the bathroom and going to the kitchen, dressed smartly in nothing but a towel.

Philip allowed himself to close his eyes while Barry took down cups from the cabinet and poured the usual amounts of coffee, half and half and sugar in the cups.

Barry's shuffle into the room was the final impetus needed to force Philip into a sitting position, as he eagerly reached out for his cup.

"Thanks, Sweetie. I told you that you were good for something."

Barry smiled and said, "Okay, what's on for the weekend?"

Philip took a sip and said, "Let's do the dinner thing tonight with the dykes, and we can maybe catch a drink at the Pub on the way home. How's that?"

"That's fine, but that's not what I meant. What about tomorrow?"

Philip was quiet as he sipped his coffee, thinking before he spoke up.

"We really need to finish doing some organizing in here. You've been here two weeks, and we're still walking around boxes."

Barry let out a sigh. "Okay, if we do some work in the morning, can we PLEASE do something fun in the afternoon? We need a little excursion."

Philip gave him a big smile. "Okay, let's do the zoo thing. You still want to see the Komodo dragon, right?"

"You're right. I almost forgot. Let's plan on that, okay? We'll visit our dragon friend tomorrow afternoon."

Philip's smile became downright lascivious as he slowly placed his coffee on the bedside table and took Barry's cup from his hand.

"What are you doing?" Barry asked. "I'm not finished."

"I thought you said you wanted to see the dragon," said Philip.

As the entendre dawned on him, Barry gave him a mischievous grin. Philip threw the sheets to the side, and Barry looked up and down his naked body through greedy eyes. He smiled and pointed.

"What's that?"

Philip glanced south. "That's my pet dragon. Wanna play with him?"

* * * *

The crash was so sudden and so loud that Jerry spilt his coffee all over himself and his Saturday morning paper.

"God DAMMIT!" he cried, rising from his chair and trying not to drip coffee onto the fabric. He walked into the kitchen with his hands held away from his body, as though he would die if the coffee touched his clothes.

"That stop sign is going to kill somebody one of these days. If it doesn't kill me first!"

Jerry finished washing his hands and hurried to the living room, where he pulled aside the drapes to see the latest victims of the villainous French Quarter Stop Sign travesty.

"I'm not going out there until I'm sure that no one's going to pull a gun," he muttered to himself. "You just can't be too careful these days."

Jerry looked back and forth as he surveyed the carnage. He glanced up and down the street to see if there was anything untoward happening…other than the damaged vehicles stuck in the intersection, that is.

This one's not too bad, he thought, as he observed three people circling the two automobiles that had been involved in the accident—a Subaru and a Trans Am.

This one should be easy to read, thought Jerry, who had his own theories about certain cars—why people bought them and how to identify their owners. "Two dykes and a straight man with a small penis," he said out loud.

He smiled as he took a closer look at the unfortunate victims…two women, and the fact that they were looking disgustedly at the sport utility vehicle confirmed the assumption that the Subaru belonged to them. The other person involved in the accident was a sloppy-looking blue-collar type, possibly a red neck.

With bravado and confidence, Jerry said out loud. "Hah! I was right! Well, Jer, you're two for two this morning." He took a closer look at them.

The man looked to be in his late thirties, with a broad-chest and an even broader middle, and no butt. This latter feature—or lack thereof—was highlighted every thirty seconds or so, at which time he would adjust his pants, pulling them well above his waistline. It was a losing battle, as the pants shimmied lower and lower with each step that he took until they finally rested low on the upper part of where a butt should have been.

Jerry smiled and shook his head from side to side, chuckling. "Poor fellow. I wonder how he can even find the damn thing with that belly hanging over it."

Jerry was momentarily distracted by the rubber neckers driving by. Since the accident occurred right at the intersection, cars were having a great deal of difficulty getting around them. Of course, they all had to take a peek as they were passing.

Four tea dance queens passed in a convertible, the top down and the music blaring.

"I'm too sexy for my shirt, too sexy for my shirt, so sexy it huuuuurts!"

"Well, those lyrics are appropriate," said Jerry. He craned to get a better look at the guys, who were shirtless and sporting both muscles AND tans.

"Ohhh, come to Daddy."

This car of gay men was followed by another…and then another.

"A royal caravan, full of queens," muttered Jerry.

The man—who was obviously at fault, by the way—was getting a wee bit uncomfortable with all of the attention. Jerry noticed that the guy had been watching the people as they passed, and that his face adopted a progressively distraught look as he realized that he was surrounded by sissies and bull daggers.

Just then, a drunk queen rounded the corner, probably just on his way home after a long, late-night shift. It was pretty obvious that he had a few drinks in him from the way that he was weaving down the street.

He had probably been looking at the scene for a minute or so as he was walking down the street, and in his drunken state of mind, he had undoubtedly decided it to be some civic duty to make some comment on the situation. He fairly careened as he drew near to a pole that was on the corner, trying to avoid it while making the turn and looking back at the accident scene at the same time.

He slowed down a bit as he turned to face the scene and those involved in it. With a grand gesture, he waved his arm a bit wildly in the direction of the Trans Am man and said, matter-of-factly, "Love that tee shirt, baby, but those pants gotta go."

He didn't say it with a smile, but rather as though his assessment of the man's attire was a matter upon which he had been consulted. After his fashion pronouncement had been made—and bitterly digested by its target—he resumed his drunken promenade down the street.

Jerry laughed as he watched the scene unfold.

"Oh, this is too good. I just gotta share this with somebody."

He went back into his bedroom, grabbed the cordless phone and dialed a number as he walked back to his observation post by the window.

"Who's this? Barry? Is Philip there? No, I don't have to talk to him, just get your butts to the front door and check out this commotion at the corner…you heard it, too? Hell, the whole Quarter did…nearly burned my damn hands with hot coffee when it scared the shit out of me…C'mon over, we can watch it from my window and have some coffee…"

Jerry realized how silly it was—rude and tasteless, even—to make sport of someone else's tragedy, but he justified his glee with the knowledge that no one was hurt in the accident.

He heard movement on the sidewalk, and assuming that Philip and Barry were on their way over, he went to the door to let them in. Instead, what he heard was a shout from Philip.

"Omigod! Are y'all okay?"

* * * *

"I just can't believe this happened! This damn sign is driving everybody crazy!" said Linda, waving towards the intersection.

Philip nodded, taking in the scene that Jerry had described moments earlier.

He said, "Well, the city, in its infinite wisdom, thought this was a good idea, so go figure."

The other woman had been inside of the Ford. She got out and slammed the door shut.

Philip leaned over and kissed her gently on the cheek. "I'm sorry, hon. Maybe this doesn't help much, but at least you're not hurt. Besides, now I know that the rumors are true: You ARE still dating," he added with a smile.

Patricia looked over at Linda, whose eyes were beginning to swell with tears. Patricia walked over and gave her a hug.

"It's okay, Linda."

Linda quietly sniffled against Patricia's shoulder for a moment, then pushed away quickly and dabbed her eyes with a tissue she had been holding. She took a deep breath and said, "I just can't believe it. I just bought this damn thing after driving around in that old car for all those years. And this happens!"

Barry appeared and walked towards them.

"Everybody okay?" he asked.

Linda answered, "Yeah, we're fine. Just a little shaken up."

"Coffee's ready," yelled Jerry from his doorway. "Who wants a cup?"

"I could sure use a cup, buddy."

All heads turned to see who had been the first to take up Jerry on the offer. It was the redneck.

There was an awkward silence for about two seconds, but Jerry recovered like a pro. Not missing a beat, he sported his most nelly stance and dialect.

"Sure, darlin', I'll give you a cup. But I should warn you that I think I dropped one of my eyelashes in the coffee. Let's pretend it's a baby and it's a king cake party." Then he squealed and posed against his door jamb.

* * * *

The streetcar jostled its passengers gently from side to side, lulling them into a near slumber with the hum of its wheels on the worn tracks. Joel was fighting to keep his eyes open, because he wanted to be awake in case something interesting happened on the streetcar…and something interesting almost always did. He had decided that this was his favorite pastime as of late. The streetcar provided an excellent forum for the study of characters.

Joel had decided that he would take the streetcar at any opportunity, and since he had spent the afternoon walking around the quarter, he knew that he would be in for a show…especially since Jazz Fest had just ended. There were a lot of characters that seemed to have decided that they would stay in town just a little bit longer than they had originally planned.

Of course, Joel was keenly aware of the fact that he was procrastinating terribly. Exams were less than a week away, but he was having difficulty forcing himself to sit down and study. Ever since he had come out—last semester—he was constantly fighting the urge to up and go to the Quarter. He wanted to experience everything that he could about himself. He felt so free, so liberated. The Quarter provided such a nice distraction.

Another reason he needed a distraction was because Lance was really getting on his nerves. It was bad enough that Joel was dealing with being gay, but now that Lance was beginning to realize that he was gay too, the tension in their relationship was mounting. They were still having sex like rabbits, but Joel had a strong sense that Lance didn't feel the same way for him. It was quickly becoming a one-way relationship, and Joel knew it.

But the streetcar has the power to make me laugh and forget.

Just when he thought it was going to be a boring trip, they squealed to a stop at Lee Circle. The driver looked weary as he swung the door open for the new passengers. First, there was a thirtyish straight couple and their seven-year-old son. Next up the steps came a couple of worn queens, probably in their mid-sixties. They were followed by two men and a woman in their early twenties who looked like leftovers from the '60s: Long hair, hippie clothes—the whole bit.

The driver closed the door, and the new passengers slowly made their way deeper into the car. Their footsteps were jerky as they tried to steady themselves while the streetcar threw them off balance. The couple and child waddled back to the area in which Joel was sitting. The seat across the aisle from him was empty, and the man looked at his wife, inclining his head slightly in the direction of the seat and raising his trimmed blond eyebrows, looking for some kind of approval. Her response was a terse and quick nod of the head. She seemed more worried about the safety of her son. She was clutching his little hand so tight that her knuckles were an odd pale color. Her son looked up at her constantly, aware that his parents were a bit uneasy in this environment, but not sure why.

Joel didn't realize that he had been staring until he locked eyes with the father.

The man smiled at Joel, pleased that he had managed to catch his attention without having to be too forward.

He gave Joel a big smile, showing a very large set of teeth that somehow matched his thinning blond hair. Joel stifled a laugh.

I've never seen anyone with blond teeth.

"How arrr ya?" the man asked, rather loudly.

Joel jumped a bit, not because the voice was loud, but because it was spoken with a grating Midwestern accent. Joel imagined what it would be like to be transported into a scene from Fargo or Lake Woebegone.

Nah. I don't think there are streetcars in Minnesota.

"Is anybody sitting herrrre?"

Joel wasn't aware that he had become responsible for seating arrangements in the streetcar.

Boy, those Midwestern "r's" are so sharp that they hurt.

"Uh, no sir. Help yourself," Joel answered.

"Thanks," said the man, who indicated to his wife that she should get a seat by the window. She fairly dragged her son in front of her and then quickly seated him on her lap.

No sooner had she sat down than she turned to stare at the two queens who had been walking behind her.

Joel followed her gaze. These guys were worthy of stares. The first one had a stern look, accented by a little ponytail pulled so tight that his face had Asian qualities.

The man behind him was a little younger, maybe in his forties, much slimmer and with his hair in a kind of bun. Both of them had hair with that freshly dyed look. Jet black. Very unnaturally jet black—black as a wet seal wading in from the ocean.

They had been whispering to each other as they made their way to the back, but they had become strangely silent after the Minnesota dialogue had begun. But as they passed Joel's seat, they both became suddenly animated as their eyes focused on the man who was sitting behind Joel.

The man with the bun pointed at the man sitting behind Joel. "Petunia?"

Joel had not paid much attention to the guy sitting behind him, because he had been on the streetcar already when Joel boarded and because he had been very quiet the entire time. Now he suddenly came to life, like a doll that had just been wound up after lying in the corner unnoticed for years.

"Hey, girl, yeah! What are y'all doin'?"

"Shoppin'," said the ponytail. "How you?"

"Good! Y'all come sit here." said Petunia, indicating the seat that was across the aisle from him and right behind the Minnesotans.

Joel had the distinct feeling that he was in for some entertainment. He had to fight the urge to turn completely around to get a better look. Instead, he scooted all the way to the corner next to the window and sat at an angle so that he could at least get an occasional peek at the show.

Bun and Ponytail had a seat. Almost simultaneously, they began brushing their clothes down, as though they were wearing skirts and wanted to make sure that their panties weren't showing.

"Where are y'all goin' shoppin'?" asked Petunia, who scooted a little closer to the aisle to chat with his companions.

"Honey, we started at Krauss." said Bun. "I needed some new shoes, girl. They don't make heels like they used to."

The Minnesotans began to squirm.

"You right, sistuh," said Ponytail. "And Missy here needs to go to Krauss for those big feet she got."

Bun spun around in her seat and glared at Ponytail. "Listen, queen, don't get me started. I'll tell everybody about how we had to go down Dryades Street and ask those black ladies to fit you in a corset."

The hippies were oblivious. The Minnesotan couple kept trying to keep the little boy's head facing forward, but he was fighting to do what Joel wanted to do—stare right at these "queens" and get a good look.

The drag queens were giggling at the corset bit. There was a slight lull in the conversation as the little boy finally spoke up. "Mommy, is she really a queen?"

The Midwesterners got off at the next stop. Long after they had disembarked, everyone else was still laughing.

* * * *

Lance ran his hands through his thick blond hair yet another time.

God, why does he keep doing that? Joel asked himself. Impatiently glaring at his friend, he sat at his desk, his arms crossed and his foot tapping the floor.

Lance was the strong silent type, but Joel was amazed at how fragile he was when they were together. It would be fair to say that Lance had allowed Joel to know him like no one else did. And Joel knew that it made Lance nervous to be vulnerable.

Lance's thoughts were racing. Just a few months earlier, he had faced feelings that he had been aware of all of his life, but which he had somehow managed to keep deep within his psyche. Then Joel came along.

Lance had always been the big guy on campus. Not especially intelligent, but smart enough to get himself into a good university like Tulane. Of course, he sometimes thought, that big donation his father made probably didn't hurt matters any.

Still, Lance was accustomed to being the center of attention…and for good reason. Standing a good six feet, with blond hair, a tan, and still rippling with the muscles he had attained during an active sports career in high school and maintained with a regimen he kept faithfully at Tulane's gym. Joel also assumed that the wealth of Lance's family made him even more attractive to women.

Girls had always been readily available for Lance; in fact, they were usually crawling all over him. When he had finally confronted his homosexuality, he found himself wondering why he had not realized it before. He didn't have a good reason, except for the fact that maybe the girls kept him so busy that he didn't really have much time to think about anyone else. Most of all, he realized, it was fear of his father that kept him from feeling anything at all. Anything but fear, that is.

But feeling was exactly what he was doing at the moment, and it wasn't a pleasant experience. Right now he was confronting the complexities of his relationship with Joel. This entire semester, they had been living as lovers. The fact that they had been roommates since their freshman year had kept people in the dark about the evolving nature of their relationship. It seemed to Lance like everything had been going just fine until Joel had to become more and more open about his being gay.

Joel just doesn't understand! He got into Tulane on a scholarship, because he is so damned smart. It doesn't matter if HE is gay or not. But me, I'll get cut off from my family, from the money, from everything!

More distraught than ever, Lance ran his hands through his hair again, this time halting as he pulled his hair back, leaving his bangs taut and flat against the top of his head.

Joel had been watching him suffer in silence long enough.

"Lance, would you quit? You're going to go bald if you keep that up."

At the sound of Joel's voice, Lance started, looking up and letting his hands fall into his lap. He glanced down at the floor for a second and then looked back up at Joel.

"Joel, could I have some time alone…for awhile to…to do some thinking?"

Joel let out a sigh of exasperation. He had to admit that he was feeling frustrated—even angry—with Lance right now, but he also couldn't help being concerned about the man who was, after all, his best friend as well as his lover.

Joel straightened up from his seated position and slapped his hands lightly on his lap.

"Okay, baby," he said, standing up. He wasn't sure, but he thought he saw Lance wince when he said "baby."

"I've got to check the mail, anyway," he continued, trying not to be overly concerned. "Then I'll pick us up a coupla Cokes. How's that?"

Lance opened his mouth, but Joel silenced him with his right hand. "I know, DIET Coke, you don't have to tell me."

Lance responded with a weak smile. "Thanks."

Joel looked at his watch as he walked toward the door. "I'll be back in…say…twenty minutes. How's that? Enough time?"

Enough for me to think? No. Enough time to jump out of a window? Probably. "Yeah, that's fine."

The door closed with a gentle thump.

Thank God he's gone. But my problem isn't. But he'll be back. And my problem will never go away.

* * * *

Joel pushed hard on the glass door leading out onto the sidewalk. The early summer heat was already fierce, causing him to sweat almost immediately. He picked up his pace as he headed for the nearest vending machine, but then he slowed down, remembering that he was supposed to be taking his time.

Taking my time. Damn. Time is valuable right now! We only have one more day before Lance goes home!

Joel had lucked out, getting a job at a small antique shop on Magazine Street. He knew that they had only hired him because they were friends of Philip, but he took the job anyway, grateful for the chance to be in the city that he had come to love. And grateful, as well, to be away from his boring hometown and his parents' oversight.

He decided to find a place to sit, so he headed toward Gibson Hall, figuring that, with classes over, he should have no problem finding a place to sit anywhere on the campus.

He plopped down on a bench and slouched.

The past year's panoply of events rushed through his mind. This was the second year of college he had completed, so the subtle feeling of depression didn't surprise him. He knew that it came from the abrupt end of the hysteria involved in completing the semester's work. But the depression was a little different this year. He was about to say good-bye to his first lover. The question was, "Is this good-bye for the summer or good-bye for life?"

A sudden tightness in his chest caused him to grimace. He leaned forward and rested his elbows on his knees.

Why can't he just come out like I did? Why does he have to hide? So what if his parents find out and cut him off?!? I could tell my parents, too. We'll be happy.

Joel pondered.

Would we be happy?

He knew that Lance loved him, but he also knew that Lance was incapable of loving him openly, and that mattered a great deal to him right now.

The pain returned to his chest with a surge. Joel straightened up, rubbing his hand hard against his ribs, trying to ease the pain.

I love him so much. I don't know what I'd do without him.

Tears began to well up in his eyes. No matter what their relationship had become, Lance had been Joel's friend for two years. And even though Lance came across as a dumb jock, Joel knew that when they were alone during those most intimate of moments, Lance was the most gentle of souls.

The tears were blurring his vision now.

I can't stand the thought of not being able to touch him, to hold him. How can he do this to me? How can he love me but push me away?

A tear rolled down Joel's cheek, and as he brushed it away, he looked around him to make sure that no one was around. Barely a soul.

I've got to hold on. I've got to be with him.

In a room across campus, someone else was in torment, thinking, *I've got to get out of this. I just can't do it anymore. I can't deal with it.*

Despite their differences, there was one thought that they shared: They were still best friends, and still in love.

* * * *

When Joel walked into the room, he was surprised to see Lance in the same position he left him, with his head in his hands. Joel walked over to him and stroked his hair lightly, wishing he could take away some of his anxiety.

"Lance, we're going to be okay. Don't worry."

Lance responded by shaking his head free of Joel's hand, crossing his arms and leaning back. Bad body language, he thought, immediately regretting casting off Joel so lightly. When he looked up at Joel, he wasn't surprised to see an injured look on his face.

God, he's so sensitive.

He reached out to grab Joel's hand and brushed his lips lightly against it. He heaved a great sigh and looked up into Joel's eyes.

"Joel, I love you."

Joel smiled down at him.

"But," he continued, taking a big pause, "I think it's best that we not see each other anymore."

Joel's summer was not going to be a pleasant one.

* * * *

The Pub was crowded, but Philip had managed to commandeer a coveted corner table, so he and Barry were able to avoid the elbows and shoulders of the roiling crowd. They were people-watching, a favorite pastime of theirs.

Philip gasped. "Okay, don't look yet, but I think that the creepy guy in the red shirt is feeling up the guy next to him!"

Barry, of course, immediately turned to look. "I think you're right. I'm not sure if the other guy is sober enough to notice."

Philip smirked. "Oh, he knows he's getting groped, but he is probably drunk enough to think that creep is sexy enough to let him do it."

Barry noticed that a man was making his way toward their table. "Hey, Philip, isn't that your friend coming up behind you?"

Philip turned to look, then popped up from his stool, grinning.

"Hiya, DaShawn! I was hoping I'd see you tonight." Philip gave him a big hug. "You remember Barry?"

"Of course," he said as they shook hands. "Just making my rounds, seeing if I was missing anything."

"Nothing much," said Philip. "You've seen me, so it's all downhill from here."

DaShawn laughed. "I guess so. I think I'll head down to Wolfendale's for a drink before I go home. Y'all want to join me?"

Philip and Barry didn't reply at first. They looked at each other, wondering if they were thinking about the same thing. Barry cleared his throat.

"I guess I'm still kinda new around here, but I thought Wolfendale's was exclusively African-American."

DaShawn was prepared for this. "Yeh, that's what everybody thinks. It is kind of a black bar, but it's not like you have to be black to get in."

"We didn't mean that," Philip chimed in, concerned that he was going to be pegged a racist. "I just thought they—you—gay African Americans wanted to have your own space."

DaShawn laughed. "Y'all are hilarious. You look terrified! One night, I'm dragging both of you down there with me."

"Really?" Philip perked right up. "What about tonight? C'mon, Barry, let's take a walk on the wild side! Lead the way, DaShawn!"

DaShawn shook his head and chuckled.

This oughta be interesting…

* * * *

Sky

The shutters flew open and landed with a thud, banging against the wooden siding on the front of the little antique shop on Magazine Street. The birds seem a little too happy, thought Joel, as he slammed the window shut. He pulled the curtains back together, surprised that the brief opening of the window had caused the temperature there to rise a couple of degrees.

He repeated the routine on all of the windows: the other three facing Magazine Street, then two on each side of the Victorian house that had been converted from a double shotgun house into a retail shop a few years earlier.

Joel was just getting the hang of things. He had only been working at the store about two weeks, not long after the spring semester had ended. The owner, Sky, already trusted him enough with the keys to the place.

"Of course, he trusts me," he said to himself. "He'd do anything to not have to show up here at nine o'clock in the morning."

He smiled to himself, admitting that he didn't mind working at all. He had met Sky through Philip, who didn't waste any time trying to find Joel a job for the summer. Meeting Sky and his lover of many years, Steve, had made Joel feel all the more welcome in New Orleans.

It wasn't that he needed to feel welcome, really; after all, he had been attending Tulane for the past two years. But he had come to feel so free with the fact that he was gay, even though it had been less than a year since he had finally admitted it to himself—even less time since he'd been in a relationship with Lance.

Joel felt his chest tighten, as the pain from his stomach moved swiftly up his torso and ended in an acute pain near his throat.

He closed his eyes and took a deep breath.

Damn! I was feeling so good until I started thinking about him.

Their last day together was horrid. Joel recollected fleeting images of that day: Lance packing in silence, averting his eyes every time he looked in Joel's direction, the cold hug good-bye...

Joel opened his eyes and tried to shake off the feeling of loneliness that was creeping back. He knew that his feelings for Lance would take a while to disappear. If only they had put some closure on their relationship, he might feel better, but Lance had preferred to let things hang, saying, "It's best that we not see each other anymore."

What did he mean when he said that?

Joel imagined that if he had asked Lance that very question, his only response would have been to shrug and turn away.

He resumed the routine of opening the shop, busying himself as much as possible to avoid thinking about Lance. About ten o'clock, he heard the little bell at the front door tinkle. He looked up.

"Good morning, young man!" Sky sparkled, giving Joel a big smile. "You mean you haven't sold out yet this morning?"

Joel feigned shock. "You wouldn't believe it! The place was packed just a few minutes ago."

Sky gave him a big smile. "I'm hoping you saved some coffee for me."

As Sky passed him on the way to the kitchen, Joel involuntarily inhaled deeply. The sweet smell of soap and shampoo filled him with a sweet sorrow. He wondered what it was like, being in a relationship for years with the same man, settled down. Sky's lover Steve was an attorney, who did pretty well from what Joel had heard people say. Of course, he had also heard that Sky wasn't all that bad off, either. This little shop barely made ends meet, but he had it from a good source that Sky had a trust fund that he worked expertly…as least well enough to put a hefty down payment on the house they owned together on Philip Street in the Garden District.

Joel walked over to the cabinet behind the register where they kept some old rags permanently permeated with the smell of furniture polish. Sky had not asked him to do so, but he felt like a lay-about if he wasn't doing something. He didn't want Sky to think that he was lazy.

"Thank God somebody has some initiative this morning." Sky walked over to where Joel had just begun polishing a table in the front room, or "the showroom," as Joel called it. "I think I may just sit back and drink coffee today. I think that's about all I can manage."

He took a seat in a nearby rocking chair and sipped his coffee.

Once again, the masculine essence of Sky's cleanliness filled Joel's nostrils. He noticed, with some discomfort, that he was getting turned on by the smell. Sky was a lot older than he was, but he was very handsome. What Joel liked most about him was his gentle nature. He could easily imagine himself making coffee for Sky for the rest of his life.

"What's it like…you know, being with someone for so many years?"

Sky was surprised by the question. Joel was a little surprised himself that he had blurted it out like that.

Sky cleared his throat and pursed his lips. "Well, let me think…being with someone is great. Being with someone for many years is another story altogether," he said, smiling at Joel as he did so. He expected this answer would be sufficient, but when he noticed that Joel was still looking at him, it was obvious he was anticipating more.

Sky took another sip of his coffee and tried to think about what his relationship was like after so many years.

"You know, Joel, being in a relationship is great, but it's not always that way. It's not a black and white thing. Know what I mean?"

Joel was thinking hard. "I guess…no, not really. I mean, you either love somebody or you don't, right?"

Sky gave him a patronizing smile. "Spoken like a true teenager in love."

Joel frowned. "I'm twenty, remember?"

Sky chuckled, making a mental note that he needed to be careful about some of his comments. There had been other occasions when he had made lighthearted, teasing remarks and Joel had taken them all too seriously.

"Sorry, but still, twenty is young when it comes to love."

"What do you mean?"

Sky leaned back further in the chair, settling in for what could be a long one. "Okay, think of it this way. Do you love your parents?"

Joel wasn't sure if that was a rhetorical question or not, but when the silence grew by the second and Sky's face retained a quizzical look, he blurted out, "Yes, of course."

"Okay, well…good. But have you always loved them?"

Joel thought for a second, "I think so, but God knows I don't like them sometimes."

Sky leaned forward and slapped his knee.

"Exactly! Love relationships are also like that. Steve and I love each other very much, but we do have our bad days."

Joel resumed polishing the table. "Lance and I…well, it's hard for me to compare our relationship with the way I love my parents."

Sky shook his head, agreeing, "I understand what you're saying, but believe me, there is something common about all relationships, and that something is the way that our feelings can change. It's not that we stop loving, but that the way we love and how much we love may change. See?

"I guess so."

In truth, Joel did not understand. He knew one thing—he missed Lance and wanted to be with him. Right now. Unless, of course, he could find someone like Sky.

For the rest of the day, Joel kept himself busy so that he could get his mind off of Lance. He was surprised when Sky called out that it was closing time. Part of him wanted the day to last longer, because he dreaded being alone in the evenings.

Sky turned off the lights in his office.

"Ready to head out?"

"Sure. Hey, do you want to come work out with me today?"

Joel asked Sky this question nearly every day, but Sky had taken him up on it only once. One glorious time. Joel thought Sky looked very sexy when he was sweaty and stripped down.

Sky looked a little uncomfortable as he thought about an answer. It wasn't overt, but Joel could sense it.

"No, thanks, Joel. I think I'll go for a run with Steve when he gets home from work. I feel so old when I go to Tulane. It's bad enough being my age, but being my age naked with other guys…man, that was really scary."

Joel shook his head, "No way, Sky. Your body is really hot."

Joel couldn't believe he had blurted that out, and he felt the blood rush to his temples. He thought about the shower room and the rush he always got from seeing a man naked behind a mysterious, thin veil of steam. The image was getting him aroused.

Sky was doing his own blushing, but he seemed flattered. "You think so?" he asked almost bashfully, looking over at Joel. "Or are you just saying that because I'm your boss?"

Joel laughed. "Hell no! You really *do* have a great body. I mean, you're not that old anyway."

"When *you're* this close to forty, you'll know how it feels, don't worry."

Joel was quiet while he picked up his backpack and slung it over his shoulder. "You make it sound like you're ancient or something," he said. "Anyway, age doesn't matter to me."

He shifted the position of his backpack and looked at the floor. He really didn't want to go home alone.

"Are you sure there's nothing else you need me to do before I leave?"

"No, that's enough for today. I'll see you in the morning, okay?"

Acting on an impulse, Joel strode over to where Sky was standing, threw an arm around his neck and gave him a long, hard squeeze, not letting go until he said, "Thanks for being so good to me, Sky."

For his part, Sky was a little shocked at this sudden display of affection. He patted Joel on the back awkwardly, nearly overcome by the sexual energy that was flowing between them.

My God, what is this? Not only am I in a relationship, but I'm almost twenty years older than this kid!

Joel let Sky go as quickly as he had grabbed him. His eyes searched Sky's, but he didn't know what he saw there.

Sky smiled and tried to act casual.

He doesn't know how dangerous the combination of youth and beauty can be.

"You're welcome, Joel. Thanks for doing such a great job."

* * * *

The window unit roared, drowning out everything else in the world and making it nearly impossible to watch television, but there were advantages of having a loud air conditioner. For one thing, it made it impossible to hear the hustlers carrying on outside on Burgundy Street—that is, except for the rare occasions when a couple would get drunk and one would throw the other against the siding. But that didn't happen all that often.

Barry looked over at the 220-volt AC unit from his reclined position on the sofa. The perspiration on his head was almost all gone, evaporated in the intense cool of the apartment. He wondered what it would be like to live in New Orleans without air conditioning. Then his thoughts wandered to more important matters.

He closed his eyes and began thinking about his life. Where was he going? Did he really like what he was doing? Did he want to be working in hotels for the rest of his life?

"An accountant in the service industry." He grunted, then rolled on his side and faced the empty television set. He hated the term "service industry." What did it mean, anyway? He didn't really serve people. That seemed to imply altruism. No, he was in it for the money, plain and simple.

His job as an accountant at a nice hotel made his life easy enough, but lately he was feeling more and more isolated from the world, and more importantly, from himself. Now in his mid-thirties, Barry was beginning to think about the rest of his life. He wanted to do something that he enjoyed doing—a job that he could find some meaning in.

Barry felt a hand lightly caress his hair. He looked up as Philip asked, "Were you sleeping?"

"Nah." He scooted over to make room for Philip. "I just got back in myself a few minutes ago. I didn't even hear you come in."

"Came in the back way," said Philip, continuing to caress Barry's hair. "I heard Darlene and Jerry grilling, so I went through the back gate to chat with them for a few minutes. We're invited, by the way."

Barry reached over to rub Philip's back, but he stopped as soon as his hand touched Philip's shirt.

"You're soaking wet!"

"It's damn hot standing in the sun." Philip began to cool himself off by pulling his tee shirt away from his chest.

"Are you happy?"

Barry had asked this question out of the blue, and it surprised Philip.

"Well…yeah. Are you?" Philip tried to keep himself from getting defensive. "I mean, why do you ask?"

Barry looked back towards the empty television while he thought about his answer.

"I feel a little bit like that TV," he said. "It's like I'm still here, but nothing's on any of the channels." He paused and glanced over at his lover, inquisitively. "Know what I mean?"

Philip smiled and leaned over to kiss Barry on the forehead.

"You're a mess. A lovable mess. Yes, I think I know what you mean. But what's going on here is a kind of mid-life crisis for you."

Barry looked offended. "I'm not that old."

Philip was always amused at how sensitive Barry was about the fact that he was a few years older. "No, really. Some gay men go through their mid-life crisis earlier than straight men do. And sometimes it lasts longer. Really. It was in a journal article."

"Just the expression 'mid-life' scares me. It's like I can hear a clock ticking, and I only have a limited time to do things."

Philip adored Barry when he was like this—vulnerable, open, honest. He brushed Barry's hair off his forehead. Barry looked up at him, and as they locked eyes, multiple emotions washed over both of them.

"It's going to be okay, sweetheart." Philip leaned in to kiss him gently on the lips. "We can talk about it whenever you want. I'm here for you."

Barry felt better already. Philip had a knack for lifting his spirits. "I forgot you were the consummate social worker. I guess I should trust you implicitly, right?"

Philip beamed, "Damn straight!"

Barry said, "Well, I know you're the professional and all, so isn't it unhealthy for you to keep wearing that wet tee shirt?"

Philip grinned. "Should I get out of these pants too?"

Barry grinned right back. "I don't care…as long as I can get *into* 'em."

* * * *

"Do you think they fight a lot?"

Darlene was asking the question as she tossed a salad in the huge silver bowl Jerry had just handed her.

"I doubt it. For one thing, they're still acting like they're on their honeymoon, and besides that, they're both so…" Jerry waved a spatula in the air, trying to find the right word. "You know…rational."

Darlene stopped tossing and gave him a dumb look. "Rational? Philip?"

Jerry laughed. "No, really. I know he can be silly and even preposterously passionate—how's that for alliteration—but he's really into communication and all that social worker garbage he picked up."

"Yeah," Darlene agreed, "and since Barry is such the strong, silent type, I can't imagine getting a rise out of him at all. Can I have another drink, Jer?"

Jerry gave her a tired look. "Would you stop being ridiculous? Like, what am I going to say? 'No, you can't have a drink?' Help yourself."

"Okay, okay," Darlene giggled. "But back to Barry. You know, those strong silent types are the ones who turn out to be wife-beaters and murderers. Wasn't Jeffrey Dahmer strong and silent?"

"I think so." The spatula stopped in midair. "You know, he was kinda cute, too, in a strange way."

Darlene shuddered then burst into hysterics. "Jerry, *you're* strange!"

Jerry clutched his imaginary pearls in shock. "Moi?"

The phone interrupted their laughter. Jerry huffed and wiped his hands on a towel, already preparing himself for a confrontation.

"If that's Philip calling to say that he's going to be late, so help me…Hello? I KNEW it! You'd better not be late! I told you…wait…say that again?"

When Darlene noticed the change in Jerry's tone, she looked over to see his face furrowed in concern. She mouthed, "What's wrong?"

He acknowledged her with a nod, but he put up a finger to hold off her question.

"Poor baby. That's so sad. We can talk about it when you get here, precious. Okay. See you in a few. Bye."

"Jerry, what's going on?"

Jerry re-folded the towel, lay it on the counter and sighed.

"Patricia's father died this afternoon."

$$* * * *$$

"Nearly all of the pews at Most Holy Name of Jesus Church were occupied. Milton Fortier was, after all, an important man in New Orleans. There wasn't much sniffling going on beyond the family pews, but that lack of emotion was not an indicator of Mr. Fortier's lack of goodness. Not at all. In fact, many of the people gathered in the church were there to pay their respects to a great man renowned for his kindness and generosity. His beneficence had influenced the lives of so many people in New Orleans, especially those from underserved populations.

It was a grand, stately funeral presided over by the archbishop with several other bishops and quite a few clergy and dignitaries in attendance. After the service, there was the traditional slow driving procession to the cemetery a few miles away. The motorcycle unit of the police department was out in force, whooshing back and forth, stopping traffic at intersections along the way.

Patricia glumly stared out of the limo window. The past few days had been a numbing blur for her. She had always been so close to her father, and she was still having difficulty imagining her life without him. He was a rare breed of man who was capable of being both strong and gentle. She knew that her brother and sister were also mourning, but as the oldest sibling, she had shared a special bond with her father.

For a long while, she sat in the limousine in silence, lulled by the rhythm of the motorcycles. It occurred to her that she had been noncommunicative for quite a while, so she took a deep breath and looked up to see Linda staring at her with a concerned look. She smiled a little to put Linda at ease, then she turned and patted her mother's knee.

"Are you holding up okay, mom?"

Constance reached for her daughter's hand and squeezed it.

"Yes, dear. As well as can be expected. I'm still in shock. I just…he was so young…"

For the umpteenth time that day, Patricia saw the tears welling up in her mother's eyes. There was a box of tissue on the seat across from them between her sister, Toni, and Linda. Patricia gestured toward it.

"Linda, would you be so kind…?"

Linda grabbed the box and handed it over.

"Here, hon."

Patricia pulled two or three tissues out and handed them to her mom.

"I'll be okay, dear. Really, I will, but thank you. I don't want to think too much about anything right now. Let's get the graveside service completed, then we can grieve properly when we have some time alone."

Linda reached over to retrieve the box of tissue.

"I'll have it right here if you need it. Don't worry, I'll be sure to take some extra tissue with me to the tomb."

Constance smiled at her. "That would be sweet of you, Linda."

Patricia glanced out the back window.

"Mom, why did Mit not ride with us?"

There was a long pause before she replied.

"I think he decided it would be easier—with the kids—to be in a separate limo."

Toni made a scoffing sound, and Constance gave her a subtle reprimanding glance.

Patricia looked back and forth at the two of them.

"Is there something I need to know?"

"Well, it's something you already know," said Toni. "Liza has a stick up her ass."

Linda stifled a laugh. She liked Toni because Toni didn't feel the need to hold back her feelings or opinions. Still, she decided a change in topic might be a good idea.

"Toni, was it hard rearranging your med school schedule?"

"Not really. Third year isn't as bad as I thought it would be. I'm almost finished my pediatric rotation, so they didn't mind if I switched things around with other med students."

"Have you enjoyed working with the kids?"

Toni smiled. "Oh, definitely. It is kind of sad, though, seeing terminally ill patients so young."

The service at the tomb was just as majestic as the funeral. Only about a hundred people had joined the caravan from the church, so disbanding, saying goodbyes, and receiving condolences would not take too long.

Patricia whispered to Mit, "I need a little air. Would you mind if I stepped away for a while?"

Mit looked at her with concern. "Of course not. Are you okay?"

"Oh yes." She waved away his concern. "Really, I just feel like I need to get out of the crowd for a bit."

Mit looked at Linda and smiled. "I'll leave you in Linda's capable hands."

"I'll keep an eye on her," said Linda. She wasn't sure, but she thought Mit's wife had taken a tighter grip on his arm.

She led Patricia through the waning crowd to a little space between two other large tombs where they could be out of the flow of foot traffic. When she was sure that no one was within earshot, Linda asked, "What's going on? You're not the 'fainting' type."

Patricia gave her a gentle, reassuring smile. "I'm fine. It's just, you know, family stuff."

"What are you talking about?" Linda asked. "Your brother and sister are so good to you."

Patricia chuffed. "They're not the problem. It's my sister-in-law. What a prig."

Linda nodded. "She does seem a little uptight. And I don't know if she understands lesbianism, because she acts like I'm trying to steal her husband."

Patricia managed a bigger smile. "I think my brother has a little crush on you. Obviously, I can't blame him, because you were by far the most beautiful woman in church today. Did you not see the way that people were staring at you?"

Linda tried not to laugh out loud. "Girl, they were just trying to figure out why there was a black woman sitting in the family pew."

"Well, you are a part of my family. Besides, I think it's fun to keep people guessing. And just ignore Liza. Toni and I certainly try to." She took a deep breath and put her arm through Linda's. "Well, back into the fray, shall we?"

Just as they arrived back at the tomb, Constance was saying goodbye to the last of the hangers-on. As Patricia neared, her mother touched her on the cheek.

"Are you okay, dear? Mit said you weren't feeling well."

"I'm fine mom. Just needed a little air. Are you ready to go home?"

"Yes, just family will be there. We'll have something to eat. Linda, you're coming, yes?"

"Of course, if that's okay."

Constance squeezed her arm and smiled. "Of course it is, dear. And be sure to invite the rest of your family. They're waiting for you."

Patricia was puzzled. "Who? What family?"

Constance looked over Patricia's shoulder and inclined her head. "Over there. As you call them, your 'other family.' Your chosen family."

Patricia turned to see Jerry, Philip, Barry, Sky, Joel, and Darlene standing near the cemetery entrance, waiting for them.

"Toni can ride home in the limo with me. You go talk to your friends. And since they are also 'family,' be sure to invite them to the house. Believe me, there's enough to go around."

"Thanks, Mom."

Linda applied a gentle touch to Constance's back. "Are you sure you're okay?"

"I'll be fine, dear. Toni will be with me. I'll see you at the house."

Linda watched her as she joined arms with Toni and made her way to the limousine.

Such a fine, beautiful and gracious woman.

She turned around, now surrounded by the loving arms of her friends.

* * * *

Steven & Sky

"What do you mean, he 'hugged' you?" Steven asked, lines of concern spreading all over his face.

Sky shifted his place on the sofa, feeling like a ten-year-old boy who had just been caught peeking into the girls' bathroom.

"I mean just that. And *only* that," replied Sky, looking at Steven square in the eyes with conviction.

Steven persisted, not in the least bit satisfied. "Don't you think that's a little weird? I mean, he's a nice kid and all, but it's not exactly professional to go around hugging your boss."

"So what if it isn't?" Sky was getting a little defensive. "So what if people went around hugging their bosses? Maybe the world would be a better place. But that's not the point, Steven. You know as well as I do that Joel is just coming out. And to him, being gay supersedes all former models of propriety."

Steven looked dubious about this explanation. "I'm a lawyer, not a sociologist. What the hell are you talking about?"

Sky gave him a dirty look. He had attained his Bachelor's degree in sociology, but had decided against grad school. Every now and then, he knew that Steven liked taking a shot at him regarding their different levels of education.

"What I'm talking about, Mr. Hot Shot Lawyer, is that Joel sees other gay people as being part of this huge, loving family. Or like a secret society. And just like you wouldn't consider it unusual to walk up to your Mom and give her a kiss at work, even if she is your boss, neither does Joel."

Sky sat back and looked at Steven's expression, which hadn't changed much—but it HAD changed. Sky knew that he had convinced him.

Steven looked long and hard at his lover. Could he trust Sky? Of course he could! They had been in a monogamous relationship all of these years. Steven didn't think that a boyish college student could derail their relationship.

"It's not that I don't trust you, Sky, but when you first told me, I guess it was such a surprise that I overreacted."

Sky smiled. "You think YOU were surprised? I almost fell down and broke that ugly Victorian divan. You know, the one that I paid too much for."

Steven shook his head, smiling in return. "It's okay if you break it by falling on it. You've got insurance. Just don't break it doing you-know-what. We don't have insurance for relationships."

* * * *

"I miss you, Lance," said Joel. The phone grew heavy in his hand as he listened to Lance explain why he was unable to visit for the weekend. It was the middle of the summer, and Lance had managed to evade him since the end of the semester nearly two months ago. Of course, at that time, Lance told Joel that he wanted to break off the relationship completely. That ascetic, fasting approach to ending a relationship changed as soon as Lance got home and had to start dealing with his father again. Joel was more than just a boyfriend to Lance. First and foremost, Joel was Lance's best friend.

"Lance, be honest with me. Are you going to visit me at all this summer? Just tell me."

For a long time, the only sound from the earpiece was some goofy music about "that's not my baby daddy" or something like that. Lance had been quiet for so long that Joel was beginning to focus on the lyrics of the song.

"I don't know, Joel. I really don't know." Then Lance added a bit louder, with anger building in his voice, "Why do you have to pressure me all of the time? What do you want from me?"

The phone felt like an anvil in Joel's hand.

"I only want in return what I give you, Lance. A little caring, understanding, maybe affection. I don't know! I just want to feel a part of you…touching a part of me. I don't know, okay?"

There was a long, dreadful silence on the other end until Joel heard someone else's voice in the background, suddenly replacing the sound of the music, which had abruptly switched off. The voice was in the distance, but Joel could hear it.

"Why do you listen to this garbage? There's some work around the yard that I want to talk to you about. Who's that you're talking to?"

Lance answered him, but Joel thought the voice only resembled Lance's. It was both that of a small, frightened child and that of a gay man trying incredibly hard to be butch. And succeeding, Joel had to admit.

"Uh, nobody, Dad."

A stern answer came quickly from his father. "Are you just holding the phone for no reason? Who the hell is it?"

Lance's voice seemed even smaller. "It's just Joel, Dad."

"He's a good kid. Smart. Works hard, I bet. He needs to rub off on you. Tell him to come visit." And just like that, he was gone. Joel heard the door slam.

Joel's animosity toward his friend began to melt. He knew how scared Lance was of his father.

Lance was from a wealthy family and enjoyed all of the privileges that came with wealth. He also inherited the burdens, the greatest being his father.

Lance returned his attention to Joel. "You heard?"

"Yeah, I heard. Are you okay?"

"I guess so. I better go. He'll be back in here soon if I don't. And hey, it was his idea—why don't you come visit me here?"

* * * *

Lance's house was immense. It was the first place Joel had visited that, in his opinion, befitted the descriptor "mansion." At first, Lance was reticent to show him around.

"It's just a house, Joel," he said, noticing that his friend was still agog. Joel was looking up at the ceiling of the foyer, which was three stories high. Lance took the opportunity to look him up and down.

Man he looks really sexy in those shorts…

He quickly looked away, cursing himself for not being able to control himself.

"Okay, okay, I'll give you a tour."

"Wait! First, I'd like to meet your parents."

"My parents? Yeah, right. We won't be seeing them for hours. I don't think I've ever seen my dad home before 6 p.m., and my mom's at some garden party she's co-hosting."

Lance took him through most of the first floor of the house: kitchen, breakfast room, butler pantry, main dining room, two living rooms (one with a baby grand piano), library, and the back terrace overlooking a chateau-like garden and a large pool.

"Seen enough yet?"

Joel still had a faraway look on his face. "Huh?"

Lance playfully slapped his shoulder. "What's up with you? I don't think I've ever seen you quiet for this long. Except for studying, I mean."

Joel looked at Lance with new eyes. "Sorry, I just…you know, I think I understand a lot more about you now that I'm here. I mean, growing up in a place like this, what was it like?"

It was just like him to turn this experience into a learning lesson about his friend, thought Lance.

He can be so sweet. I've missed him so much.

Lance frowned. "Like I said, it's just a house. And don't get the impression that being surrounded by a beautiful house and pretty gardens means that it's a great place to live. Wealth comes at a price. You'd be surprised at how confined I felt in this place."

"Sorry," said Joel. "I know you've had some rough times here." He smiled, trying to change the mood. "Hey, let's take a break from the tour. Let's see where you hang out!"

"I stay in my bedroom most of the time," said Lance, smiling right back. Joel's happiness could be contagious. "C'mon, I'll show you."

They went up to the third floor, and when Lance opened the bedroom door, what Joel saw was more like an apartment.

"Wow," said Joel.

Lance laughed. "I wish I could go back and count how many times you've said that since you got here."

Joel gave him a sheepish look. "Sorry. It's just hard for me to imagine living in this kind of space. I had a nice bedroom, but it was just one room, know what I mean?"

Lance found himself smiling as he watched Joel stroll through the living area to his bedroom and back. Then he realized that he was looking at Joel with hungry eyes.

His tan makes him look really good, and it looks like he may have put on a little muscle. His ass looks amazing in those pants. I love the short haircut with the long bangs in front. I want to run my hands through that. And those brown eyes, so warm, so inviting, and those lips…

"Hello?" Joel was looking at him, puzzled. Lance realized that he had blindly continued admiring Joel until he was standing right in front of him.

"Huh?"

"You were just standing there looking at me funny. Do I have something in my teeth?" Joel ran his tongue across his teeth.

"Oh, no, you're fine," said Lance. He realized that he had started breathing a little harder and that his heart was beginning to pound. "It's just that you look…It's really good to see you, man."

Joel gave him a shy grin. "Glad to hear it. I've missed you."

Lance was watching Joel's lips. His luscious, beautiful lips. Lance felt something crumbling inside of him—a dam being breached by pent-up feelings. He wasn't going to deny himself what he wanted. He took a giant step forward, grabbed Joel, and put a lip lock on him. Nothing more needed to be said.

About half an hour later, they lay tangled in each other's arms, panting and enjoying the sweet afterglow. It was Joel who broke the silence.

"So, I'm guessing you missed me too."

* * * *

Two weeks later, back in New Orleans, Lance's appetite for Joel was still voracious.

"You don't actually expect us to do any studying, do you?" Lance edged a little closer to Joel and ran his hands through his hair.

Joel fought the urge to succumb and pushed him away.

"Cut it out," he said, without much conviction. "What's your father going to say when you don't do better next semester?"

At the mere mention of his father, Lance's expression morphed into a frown. He pulled his hand back as though Joel's hair was Medusa's.

"You sure know how to ruin a good mood." He was glowering at Joel.

"Hey, just two weeks ago we were at your house, and for whatever reason you decided to tell your dad that I was tutoring you. Officially, that's why he let you come down here to visit, remember?"

Lance pouted, looking at his feet.

"We've been farting around for two days," said Joel, softening up a bit. "Let's do something—anything—academic to justify your trip here. We'll have time for fun tonight at Philip's."

Lance scowled for a bit, but then he gave in with a sigh of resignation.

"By the way, I'm not crazy about spending the evening with a bunch of sissies. All right, let's work on composition. I guess I should learn how to write before I graduate."

* * * *

The aisle in Matassa's was narrow enough to begin with, but having to inhabit it with another person was unbearable.

"Stop pushing!" Barry scolded Philip, who was leaning over to get a glimpse at the rows of tomato sauce.

"I'm not pushing! You're just too big to get around," replied Philip, squeezing Barry around the waist and letting out a surprised gasp.

116

"Stop that," said Barry, looking around, concerned.

Undeterred, Philip gave him a poke in the ribs before letting up. "You're not in Dallas anymore, remember? There aren't any Southern Baptists at Matassa's, and if there are, they want to get into your pants as much as I do."

"Shhh!" Barry's face adopted a stern look. "It's not about getting caught. It's just against common decency to do stuff like that in public."

"Yeah, whatever," Philip said, giving up on amusing his frigid-in-public lover. He looked into the basket that Barry was holding. "What else do we need? We've got pasta, peas, celery, peppers, onions. We have garlic, right?"

Barry nodded.

"Tomato sauce, tomato paste. Okay. Throw in the boys we're inviting for dinner, and voila! Chicken Cacciatore!"

Barry laughed.

"Omigod! His face might crack. I believe Barry smiled. Can anyone hear me?" Philip raised his voice and gestured around the store.

"Yeah, girl, we hear you," someone hollered from the deli.

"Philip, be quiet! You're embarrassing me." Barry's face was turning crimson. He quickly made his way to the register, where a wizened little lady stood, ready to check them out.

"Y'all make such a nice couple," she said. Philip was grinning ear to ear.

Barry mumbled a "thanks" and blushed some more.

* * * *

"Mother's glass is empty." Jerry raised his glass and rattled the cubes to make his point. "Stop worrying about food and take care of what's important: keeping Mother happy."

Philip stepped into the living room—which wasn't stepping very far, since the kitchen was a mere two paces away.

"Yes, Mother," he said edging through the small crowd. "Darlene's better at serving drinks than I am. That reminds me…where is she? Anybody else ready for another margarita?"

Several glasses were immediately raised.

"These girls drink like fish," said Barry. "I'm going to have to make a third pitcher!"

Philip took a look around the room. "I think this is the largest crowd that I've ever had here."

Jerry piped up, "Not including that orgy. Before you met Barry, of course."

"Ha ha," said Philip, shooting Jerry the bird. "Anybody else wanna take a shot at me? But look out: I might spit in your plate."

He scanned the room. What a group, he thought. Sky and Steven sat on the love seat, snuggled up. He noticed that Steven kept staring at Joel.

What's going on there?

Joel sat on the floor at Lance's feet. Lance appeared more than a bit nervous, but not as bad as Philip thought he would be. Jerry presided in the lounge chair, as usual.

"Okay, Joel, you've become quite the smartass lately. I'm sure you have something to say. Go ahead and get it off your chest."

Joel looked up at Philip. "Moi? Say something bad? Now, Philip, I would never accuse you of such licentious group behavior." Joel cleared his throat. "However, Jerry has intimated that you once had quite a bit of foot traffic through here a while back."

Jerry cackled. "Foot traffic is right! A different set of shoes under the bed every night!"

Philip acted surprised. "Y'all have to stop. Barry thinks that he's the first!"

"Yeah, right," said Barry. "Maybe the first to get you into a commitment."

Quiet so far this evening, Steven surprised everyone by pitching in a comment—maybe a bit too loudly. "Question is, will you be the last?"

He was looking directly at Joel when he asked that question, and Sky elbowed him in the ribs. Philip felt a little tension in the air. It didn't take a counselor to know something wasn't right here.

Philip looked over at Joel and Lance and noticed that Lance was glaring at Steven—who was still glaring at Joel, on and off.

I'd better diffuse this little time bomb before it goes off.

"Uh, Lance and Joel, have you seen the back yard? Come on, let me show you."

Just as the chorus of "WHERE'S MY DRINK?" began, Philip yelled, "I'm going right now to get Darlene to play bartender, so chill out!"

Two minutes later, he was begging Darlene to hurry.

"I need more time," she said. "I'm not finished getting dressed! I haven't even started makeup yet."

Philip groaned. "You look gorgeous. Just slap on some lipstick. There are no straight men coming, so it doesn't matter. PLEASE, hurry! I can't make drinks like you can."

"Oh, all right. At least let me put on some earrings. I'm coming, go ahead. I'll be right behind you in a minute."

"Thanks, sweetie. You know, if I were straight, I'd marry you."

Darlene was still laughing as he closed the door behind him. When he re-joined the boys in the back yard, he could see that Lance was still agitated. He realized a little intervention might be necessary.

"Okay, Lance. I know you're upset. But please, for Joel's sake—and, quite honestly, for my sake, since it is my party—could you just let it go for now?"

"I'll try, Philip," said Lance, looking back at Joel. "But I think the guy's an asshole, and I'm not going to let him give my boyfriend any crap."

Joel looked like the happiest guy in the world. He leaned in to give Lance a kiss and, to Philip's surprise, Lance responded in kind.

Realizing that the "kiss" was going to last awhile, Philip turned to go inside.

Barry was just inside the back door waiting for him. "What's going on out there?"

"Nothing much," answered Philip. "but you would probably say it's 'against common decency.'"

* * * *

The Jeep bounced along St. Charles Avenue, jostling its passengers rhythmically from side to side. The consistent movement of the vehicle was nearly hypnotic, but it was the heat that really made the occupants sleepy.

Joel glanced over at Lance, who was driving. Joel's family wasn't exactly poor, but compared to Lance he was. Joel had always wanted a

Jeep, but he could never afford it, and his parents were far too practical to splurge on something so, so…recreational.

Of course, Lance's father wasn't exactly frivolous in his spending. But a Jeep was what Lance had wanted as a graduation present his senior year in high school, and his father said he would get one only if he attained a series of goals.

"What was it again that you had to do before your father gave you the Jeep?"

"What? How many times you gonna ask me that?" asked Lance with a smile.

Joel reached over and pinched Lances nipple. "As many times as it takes to find out what motivates you."

"Ouch!" Lance laughed and pushed Joel's hand away, "Okay, let's see. I had to make at least a 3.0 my last year, I had to score at least four touchdowns during the football season, I had to read a list of novels that he gave me—and submit to his oral examinations—plus I had to do all of the yard work that year.

"That doesn't sound so bad. I could've done that."

Lance gave him a dirty look. "Of course you could have, Mr. Brain Man. And a little yard work might do you some good."

Joel turned away from Lance and stared straight ahead. His stomach jumped a little, and a pain surged in his chest. He was becoming more conscious about the fact that Lance was so much more brawny than he was. Joel stayed in shape, but Lance would often make the kind of comment that hurt his feelings.

Lance whistled as he pointed at a gorgeous, muscled specimen jogging down St. Charles Avenue. "If you looked like that guy…Wow, man, that would be great."

Joel smiled and said, "Fuck off," then he pretended to ignore Lance by looking off to the right. He was hoping the air rushing by would dry the tears that were building up in his eyes.

* * * *

Darlene pulled the gate closed behind her and sashayed toward the back door of her apartment. Just as she was getting her keys out of her purse, she heard Philip's back door open.

"Darlene is that you? Of course it is. I'd recognize that set of keys anywhere."

"Don't make fun. These things double as a weapon in case of an emergency," she laughed, waving them in a circle as if she were brandishing a mace—the kind with the spikes on the end, not the kind you spray.

"I wish I had had a weapon like that the other day at my party. I thought I was gonna have to break up a fight with all that testosterone flying."

Darlene's mouth flew open in a gasp as she remembered the recent evening's events. "That was too much, Philip. You never did tell me the whole story. What was all that about?"

Philip took a deep breath and crossed his arms. "Okay, here's the poop. It seems as though Steven is afraid that Joel has the hots for Sky. And since Steven and Sky have been together for seven years now, I guess Steven's afraid that Sky has got the seven-year itch or something."

Darlene's mouth dropped. "You mean, Steven thinks that Sky is going to dump him for a college student. Puh-lease!"

"Love's a funny thing."

"Lust is what's the issue here, hon. Forget love."

* * * *

Jerry fiddled with his drink at the bar. Usually, when he was at Good Friends he sat near the door, but tonight he wanted to sit back and people-watch, so he took a chair near the back wall. He was just beginning to relax when something made him perk up: Joel walked into the bar and sat at a corner table with Sky. Just the two of them.

* * * *

Patricia crossed the bayou and made a right on Moss Street. Despite the late summer heat, a few joggers were out along the bayou, sweating profusely.

"That can't be healthy," Patricia said to herself. Her hand involuntarily went to her stomach, which, she realized of late, was beginning to fill in just a bit more than she wanted.

Why can't I be more like those lesbians who don't seem to give a damn about the way that they look?

She smiled slightly as she turned left onto De Soto, "Because I'm a gay man trapped inside of a lesbian body, like Philip says."

She pulled in front of her home—a little Edwardian double—and saw Linda in the front yard watering the plants. Linda waved as she drove up.

"What are you doing here?" asked Patricia, slamming the door behind her. "Did you get off of work early?"

Linda gave her a funny look. "Patti, it's after six o'clock."

"Oh," said Patricia, looking a little disoriented. "You know how I get when I'm working on a new project. I've got to have these three murals done by the end of next week."

"I know, you told me. Have time for dinner? Maybe we can pick something up at Whole Foods."

"Sounds great, but do you mind getting it? I want to get cleaned up first," she said, indicating paint stains on her arms.

"I'd be glad to," said Linda with a mischievous smile. "And, uh, clean everywhere. Just in case."

* * * *

The Corner Pocket was busy tonight, as it usually was every Friday night.

Jerry dug into his pocket for another dollar bill. He opened and shut his eyes slowly as he tried to take in the figure that was looming above him. He started with the ankles, noticing a small bracelet of some kind that was fastened there. Next he looked at the knees, which were soon swaying back and forth in front of his face. Obviously, the kid had seen Jerry digging in his pocket. Jerry smiled up into the kid's face and pulled out a wad of bills. He may have been drunk, but not drunk enough to mistakenly give the guy a five instead of a one.

The boy moved his crotch in a little closer to Jerry's face as he waved the dollar bill lamely in the air. Jerry aimed the bill at the g-string, and only with a little help from the dancer did he manage to get the bill planted. Jerry looked up and smiled at the dancer as he, in turn, gave a smile to his latest benefactor. Jerry patted him on the leg as he stood up to dance for other eager patrons waving bills in the air.

"I thought I might find you here."

Jerry turned to see the familiar smiling face of Philip, who was trying to conceal a look of concern.

"Mother needed to get out for a little while," he said, giving Philip a peck on the cheek, followed by a gentle pat with his hand.

Jerry was sitting on a stool at the bar, so Philip's vantage point allowed him to look down slightly at his landlord. It wasn't the gray hair that made Jerry look older; it was when he drinking. Philip noticed that Jerry was sweating, even though it was rather cool in the bar.

He's going to have a stroke one of these days.

"Where you going?" Jerry asked.

"Barry and I were going to do the fruit loop. You wanna come?"

Jerry leaned heavily on the bar, then turned his head to yell, "No, thanks. I'll see ya tomorrow."

Philip was worried; his friend didn't look so good. "Jerry? You okay?"

Just for a moment, Jerry's sadness peeked through his drunkenness, but inebriation took over once again. He looked back toward the dancing boy and answered, "Fine. Just needed to get out of the house for a while."

* * * *

"So…" Sky began. "Do you want to work during the semester, as well? In the fall, business usually picks up a little, so I could use some help. Especially in December."

Joel thought for a while before answering. "I could use some extra spending money, but December? I don't know. With exams and the holidays, I may not be able to work much."

Sky nodded sympathetically. "No problem, Joel. School should come first. Actually, FAMILY should come first, but I don't know if you feel that way."

"Sure I do. But you're the closest real 'family' that I have."

Sky smiled. And gulped.

"You should come with me to the Quarter Sunday," said Joel, "to see some of the Southern Decadence costumes. I highly doubt Lance wants to go. And you and I BOTH know Steven won't go. Will you come?"

"Maybe, Joel. I'll have to ask Steven."

"Do you need his permission?" Joel regretted the question, but it was too late.

Sky frowned. "No, Joel, but one day when you're in a relationship, you'll discover that you need to check with your partner before you make plans."

"Sorry," Joel said, sheepishly putting his head down. Then he looked up with a shit-eating grin. "So let's take him with us! Tonight!"

"Take him with us?" laughed Sky, infected by Joel's enthusiasm. "Take him where?"

"To the Parade! For the Big DICK contest!"

"What??!?"

Only in New Orleans, thought Sky.

* * * *

"Man, it's crowded in here tonight," said Philip, pushing his way through the crowd at Lafitte's.

"For the gay bars, Southern Decadence is now bigger than Mardi Gras," yelled Barry into Philip's ear as he tried to keep from losing him in the crowd. "I thought you knew that."

"I guess you go to bars more than I do."

Barry laughed. "Whatever. Let's go upstairs and see what Miss Thing is up to."

Philip stopped dead in his tracks. "Did you say 'Miss Thing'? Barry, before you know it, you're going to be a regular campy queen."

Barry smiled. He was in a good mood tonight, though he couldn't exactly explain why. This was his second experience of Decadence. His first occurred only a matter of days after he had moved to New Orleans, and he thought that he had died and gone to heaven. Things were going to be a little different this year, he knew, since he had a boyfriend.

The Dish, also known as "Miss Thing," was behind the bar in The Corral, snapping her fingers at some customer who was giving him a hard time. Philip walked to the bar and screamed, "Missy, I need some service."

Dish snapped his head around, ready to read someone. When he saw it was Philip, his face relaxed a bit, but the abuse spewed forth anyway.

124

"Girl! You want service? Go downstairs and talk to the dancers. Call me when you want a drink. And NOT before!"

The fingers snapped again.

Barry remained in the background, enchanted by the scene before him. The music was good, as it usually was here. Not too loud, but strong enough to make his chest vibrate a little. He observed the layer of smoke that lingered. It was hard for Barry to explain, but for some reason, smoke in any bar outside of the Quarter was nasty. Here, it seemed to belong.

The walls were filled with the requisite gay art: "Not All Men Were Created Equal," and the half-naked man in a wheat field with a scythe in his hand—that kind of stuff.

The pool table looked lonely in the middle of the room off to the side. It was crowded there, but no one was interested in playing pool tonight. A few guys in leather sat on the ledge that framed the pool room, and they were surrounded by mostly preppy-looking men who were in for the weekend.

Philip walked up and handed him a drink. "Lots of new meat in town."

"Last year," Barry commented, "I was new meat. Remember?"

"As a matter of fact, I don't remember. You and I hadn't met yet," said Philip.

"That's right. I almost forgot."

"It was the following weekend."

"When do we celebrate our anniversary, anyway?" Barry asked.

Philip took on a pensive look. "Anniversary of what? Meeting? First date? First sex? First time we had the BIG sex?"

"We haven't gotten that far yet," said Barry.

"Hmmm," Philip pondered. "Then maybe we don't have anything to celebrate yet!"

* * * *

What a difference one year can make in a man's life.

Barry adjusted his lounge chair so that it reclined a bit more. The first signs of autumn were in the air, even though it was only the middle of September.

September…

Barry thought about September of last year, when he had just moved from Dallas. He had left a lover and a life with a lover, and he had come to New Orleans feeling free and independent. He was ready to start a new life. Had he succeeded?

He leaned back and took a long draw from the glass of tea he was holding. First signs of fall, yes, but the late afternoon sun filled his back yard with an ample amount of heat. He wiped the sweat from his brow and closed his eyes again.

He was right back where he started. No, he had never left the starting gate. He sighed.

He worked in a hotel in Dallas. He works in a hotel in New Orleans. He rented an apartment in Dallas, and because he still hadn't saved enough to buy a home, he was renting a place in New Orleans. What was the difference? What was he doing with his life?

Out of the corner of his eye he saw several bees buzzing around Jerry's flowers. Barry was mesmerized by their furtive activity; they had such purpose to their work—such commitment.

They are lucky they can't realize how trivial their lives are.

The maudlin melodrama in his head made him smile, though in fact the thought sobered him.

What was the difference between his life and the life of those bees? All he did was work to put money in someone else's honey jar. No, that wasn't quite right, and he knew it. He made decent money. It occurred to him that money wasn't even the issue at all. It was meaning. *Meaning* was the issue.

Why was he here? Why was he thirty-five years old with the same career that he started at twenty-five? Why? What did he want to do? Who did he want to be?

This time Barry shut his eyes hard, as though closed eyelids would save him from the pain. No, he knew the ache was coming from way down within him, and closing his eyes wouldn't help at all. He felt a frown deepening the lines of his face, wondering if it was permanently etching sadness there.

"You can be happy now! I'm home!"

Philip sauntered into the back yard, a broad smile on his face as he drew closer to Barry.

126

The lines in Barry's face took an upward turn. Sadness was not permanent, after all.

* * * *

Jerry was in rare form, bustling about the kitchen and belting out show tunes. Philip, Barry, and DaShawn lounged in the den sipping their cocktails and cheering him on.

Jerry abruptly ended his rendition of "Anything Goes" and shouted, "Oo, oo! Let's make it a movie night! Mother is in the mood for *The Women*. Some of the best lines are from that movie."

"Uh oh," said Philip, "I have a feeling we are going to get some gay education. Pay attention, everybody! This'll be on the test."

Jerry wagged his finger at Philip. "Every word out of Mother's mouth is filled with wisdom, so you should always pay attention."

"I could always use a little gay education," said Barry. "Give us an example of a good line from the movie. Let's see if I've heard it."

"Oh, where to begin?" Jerry thought for a second, then his face lit up. "Oo! Here's one!" He strode from the kitchen into the den with his arms stretched to the left and right as though he were walking the runway, modeling a cape. He turned one way, then the other, and said, "Our new one-piece lace foundation garment. Zips up the back and no bones!"

His "audience" exchanged puzzled looks, and all three burst out laughing.

"What the hell was *that*?" asked DaShawn.

Jerry was appalled. "Wait, don't tell me you haven't seen the movie!"

"Nope," replied DaShawn between laughs. "Maybe it's some sort of white people humor I don't know about."

"No," said Barry, still guffawing. "I'm white, and I have no idea what he's talking about."

Philip was bent over at the waist, holding his stomach. "Me either! Oh, stop it, my stomach hurts from laughing so hard."

This entire time, Jerry had been gaping at them with an astonished look. Recovering, he feigned anger and approached them with an open palm.

"All three of you, turn in your pink cards right now! You're expelled from the club!" He marched over to a cabinet and started rummaging through his VHS tapes. "Okay, no one is leaving this house until we watch *The Women*."

Philip said, "Jerry, we need to go to dinner…"

"No, you don't!" Jerry cut him off. "Mother is going to cook for all three of you."

"That's sweet, Jerry," said DaShawn. "I'll be glad to stay, but something tells me I may not find it funny. If it's an old film, well…it's got white humor only."

Philip chirped up. "Hey, let's get all our black friends over here to see if they think it's funny."

"Yeah, right," quipped DaShawn. "What other black friends?"

The room grew quiet. Even Jerry stopped what he was doing to look at DaShawn.

Philip spoke up first. "What do you mean? We have black friends."

When DaShawn looked up from his cocktail, he noticed they all had terrified looks on their faces. His face broke into a smile.

"I wish you could see your faces. Y'all look like you just got accused of burning a cross in my front yard."

His three "cracker" friends relaxed a little.

"Sorry if that didn't come out right, but, chill! I'm not blaming anyone of being bigoted, I'm just pointing out something that's evident to most black people that most white people don't really think about."

"Well, Mother has to start cooking, but I am listening." Jerry placed a movie cassette by the TV then made his way into the kitchen. "Speak up so I can hear!"

"So, what *are* you talking about?" asked Philip.

"Are you serious?" asked DaShawn. "You really want to hear this?"

"Hell yeah," said Barry. "Don't leave us hanging."

DaShawn took a big sip and put his drink down. "Okay, well, think about it. When you go to a typical party in this city, how many black people are there?"

Both white boys cocked their heads for a few seconds.

"How big a party?" Philip asked.

"Does it matter?"

The white boys cocked their heads again and remained silent for a while.

"Usually just a few, I guess," admitted Barry. He turned to Philip. "Maybe one in ten?"

Philip grimaced. "Sad, but true."

"That one black guy is probably me," DaShawn chuffed. "Now, I want you to picture a 'black party' you went to. You know—a party with a black host. What was the black-white ratio?"

"Gay or straight?" Barry asked.

DaShawn wrinkled his nose. "Again, does it matter? But let's say a gay party."

There was a longer silence.

"Actually, I think it's closer to 50-50," said Philip. "Interesting."

"Do you see where I'm going with this?" Da Shawn went on, "The city is way over half black, but most white people I know only have a few black friends."

"Even gay people?"

"I think gay people may have more black friends than straight people do," said DaShawn. "But still, I think it's an issue that needs addressing."

"Okay, I wanted to ask about something," said Barry. "I think this isn't going to come out right, but I noticed that—when we were at Wolfendale's that time—a lot of the guys there were…" He stopped, unsure if he should go on.

"Nelly?" DaShawn guessed.

"Kinda, but I don't mind nelly guys or anything like that," said Barry, defensively. "I mean, it used to bother me until I stopped hating myself, but I was just wondering why it seems like a lot of the gay black guys that I saw were…flamers."

"I have noticed that," said Philip, squinting in concentration. "Now my social worker curiosity is piqued. What's the story on that?"

"Well, I don't exactly think of myself as a butch stud," DaShawn laughed. "But when I'm in that setting, I guess I look butch in comparison."

"Hey, I can be a bit 'girly' myself," said Philip, "so I'm not judging, just curious."

DaShawn leaned forward. "I may have some facts, but mostly what I have is opinion."

"Let's hear it," said Barry.

"First of all, I don't really think that there is a higher percentage of nelly black guys. If you saw some of these guys in pretty much any other setting, they might act different. It's just that they assume a different persona when they are having fun, and they feel safe doing it there. It's really noticeable if they are sharing funny stories. I mean, my friend Jerome totally transforms when he is telling a funny story. Finger snaps, squealing laughter, the whole thing."

"Aw, I know him!" said Philip. "He's a riot. How's he doing?"

"Okay, I guess. I worry about him. He likes preying on 'straight guys,' and I don't think he's always safe."

"Wow," said Barry. "I just assumed all gay guys knew better than to have unsafe sex."

"Well, he knows better, but his judgment gets cloudy when he fools around with a married man, and that's a perfect segue to the other thing I wanted to explain.

"As you probably know, attitudes about homosexuality in the black community are more negative than average. There's less acceptance, so I think that some gay black guys who can 'hide it' do exactly that: Hide it. And the ones who are…you know…more 'obviously' gay just own it and let it all hang out. But the ones in the closet aren't exactly chaste, know what I mean?"

Jerry hollered from the kitchen, "I can second that! I've heard lots of tea room stories involving really butch black guys who flee as soon as they get their rocks off."

"I'm getting the picture," said Philip. "It's not like the guys who are hiding it aren't screwing around. They're just doing it on the sly."

DaShawn nodded. "And that's one of the reasons why HIV is spreading to black women."

Barry looked confused. "Wait…where did the women come in?" As soon as he asked the question, his face registered understanding. "Oh, damn, some of these guys are married—maybe even married with kids, but they're taking it in the ass and then…"

"And then having sex with their wives," DaShawn confirmed.

There was a prolonged silence as everyone reflected on the ramifications of such behavior.

DaShawn went on, "Oh, and for some black guys in denial, wearing a condom is 'gay,' so they don't use them."

"You know, that makes sense from a psychological perspective," mused Philip. "Wearing a condom—or telling someone else to wear a condom—is a conscious acknowledgment of the sexual act."

Jerry walked into the den wiping his hands on a dishtowel. "And good luck trying to get all the leaders of the African American community in the same room to talk about it. They're in as much denial as the closeted guys." He turned back to the kitchen. "Ok, my little chickadees, I'll have something ready in about thirty minutes."

There was another silence before DaShawn said, "That's one of my goals, you know."

Philip asked, "Goals for…what exactly?"

"Sorry, I was mostly thinking out loud. Goals regarding the whole 'closeted and married and having sex with guys' thing. I'd like to do something about it."

"Tell us all about it," said Philip.

"Well, the overarching goal is to stop the spread of HIV, but one of the primary objectives is to foster more acceptance in the black community, starting with the ministers."

"Yeah right," groaned Philip. "Like Jerry said, good luck with that."

"Believe it or not," said DaShawn, "there are a few who want to be more supportive of my efforts. I've talked to a couple of them in private, and they'd like to take a more proactive approach. But they're afraid to be too vocal. And I doubt they'll ever do anything from the pulpit. They're afraid of the publicity."

"Oo!" Jerry ran back into the room, placed his hands on his face, and screamed. "The publicity! Oooo, la publicitè!!!"

There was a second of silence, and once again Jerry's audience fell into hysterical laughter.

Jerry held out his hand again and yelled at them. "Turn in your pink cards! Y'all are a disgrace to the word 'gay!'"

"Stop," cried Philip, doubled over, laughing. "You're killing us!"

Jerry pointed at the TV.

"Barry, stop your howling and pop in that tape. Now! Before I scratch your eyes out." His face lit up, and he struck another pose. Putting his arms out in front of him, he showed all of them his fingernails and screamed, "Jungle Red!"

Philip fell onto the floor.

* * * *

Joel tugged his backpack higher on his shoulders as he stepped lightly down the stairs in Gibson Hall. He had memorized which steps would make the most noise as he stepped on them. Yep, there was one…then another. The creaks had a solemn tone—more like a fart than a squeak. He smiled to himself, thinking about how ridiculous it sounded to refer to a fart as "solemn."

He rounded the corner where the stairs met the window and continued down the rest. *This is a lot like exercise*, he thought. *I wonder if my legs'll get bigger going up and down these stairs.*

Joel was really in no "need" of exercise. In fact, he exercised regularly enough—at least three times a week. But Lance had been making more and more negative comments about his body lately. No one had ever done that before. Joel thought he had a nice body. Certainly, most of the guys he met at the bars thought he had a nice body.

But then again, some of them are just plain lecherous.

Joel was learning quickly enough that there were a lot of people out there who wanted nothing more than a quick balling. Period.

And what's wrong with that? A little voice asked in his head.

Joel wanted more than that. He wanted a relationship with someone like…like Sky. But Sky was already in a relationship with Steve.

The stairs long behind him, Joel trudged across campus to his new digs. He and his, er, boyfriend? Lance had managed to get a good deal on a one-bedroom apartment just off campus. Lance's father had agreed to foot most of the bill, especially since he had such a high opinion of Joel. He thought that Joel was a good influence on Lance, and he told Joel that he could pay less rent if he continued tutoring Lance.

Joel had to smile again. If only Lance's father knew what he was teaching him after hours!

* * * *

As Jerry had expected, the bar crowd was quiet on a weeknight right after Southern Decadence. It was the same after Mardi Gras, as well.

Everyone hit the Quarter for a few days, then retreated. The bar scene was usually quiet for a few days.

Not me. No retreat for me.

Jerry raised the glass to his lips. His fingers trembled.

A retreat. A retreat from the bars. Who is the enemy?

Jerry gulped hard, his eyes stinging from the vodka he had ordered straight up. Or was it from the cigarette he left burning in the ashtray?

Jerry wiped his eyes, and the bartender came his way.

"You okay? Jer?"

It wasn't until Jerry tried to say, "I'm fine," that he realized he had been crying. It wasn't the vodka or the smoke after all.

Oh, yes it is, thought Jerry. The last thing he heard was a slight gasp from the bartender. And he probably wouldn't remember that later.

Jerry's head hit the bar.

The bartender turned around and yelled to the manager, "Dial 911!"

* * * *

The room seemed to be getting smaller to Jerry, as he sat back in his favorite chair. This was usually the place where he could be himself, where he could shut out the outside world and say "Fuck you" to whoever couldn't handle him or accept him the way that he was. But now, it seemed, the outside world had invaded his inner sanctum.

Almost as if he could read Jerry's mind, Philip said, "It's not like I'm an outsider, Jerry. Or a stranger. I'm your friend, and the only reason why I feel compelled to say these things is because I care about you."

Jerry got up from his chair, which had transformed from a place of refuge to a strait jacket. Without a word, he walked toward the hall and out of sight.

As soon as he was alone, Philip heaved a great sigh, trying to dispel the tension from his body. He was honored to be Jerry's closest friend, but it now began to dawn on him that a great deal of responsibility was on the horizon. Spending the night in a hospital room looking after Jerry was a dose of reality for which he hadn't quite prepared. Not this soon, at least.

That morning, before Philip had even provided proof that he had medical power of attorney, the doctor had taken him aside to confide in him. He said that Jerry was in bad health and that if he didn't take care of himself, he was headed for certain doom.

Why did the doctor assume he could tell me these things?

Philip admitted it seemed logical, since he was the only one who showed up—and stayed – at the hospital until Jerry was discharged. Everyone probably assumed that they were a couple, even though Jerry was Philip's senior by thirty years.

Did he think I was his son?

Philip sat back and tried to come up with a strategy on how to deal with the situation. When Jerry had not reappeared after five minutes, he decided to check on him.

"Jerry?" he called, looking first in the bathroom and then glancing toward the bedroom. Jerry didn't answer, but Philip could see part of him reflected in the mirror. He was sitting on the bed, his back to the door, facing the mirror.

"Jerry, you okay? I thought you'd gone to the bathroom."

Jerry didn't look Philip's way, nor did he answer. With a slight turn of his head, he indicated that he was aware of Philip's presence, but everything that he did *not* do indicated he would prefer to be alone.

Philip approached the bed slowly, trying to be keenly aware—and respectful—of his friend's feelings. As he drew nearer, Philip heard a sniffle, and as he looked from the back of Jerry's head and into the mirror, he could see that Jerry had been crying. Philip stopped, wanting to comfort, but trying so hard to give the man some space.

After a minute or so of silence, Jerry seemed to make a conscious decision to stop crying. He took a deep breath and reached for his handkerchief in his back pocket.

He looked at Philip's reflection in the mirror while he wiped his eyes. "It's funny. For years, the only thing I really remember crying about was my friends who had died. Now, suddenly, I cry for no reason."

"It's okay, Jer. Hell, it's good for you. Releases endorphins, or something like that."

Jerry looked down at his handkerchief, still sniffling a little. "I just don't know what's wrong with me. I just can't explain it. I used to have a wonderful life. Then I lost Gary. Then I retired. Then I…I started to go a little crazy."

He started to get up, but changed his mind. The tears began to flow again.

"I used to be a happy, put-together kind of person," he said, the words difficult to understand as his face contorted with his pain. "Then life seemed to change. I got older. I got…lonely. And then, I guess I got drunk."

Philip could hold still no longer. He walked over to the bed and put an arm around Jerry's shoulders, which began to shake uncontrollably at the touch of another human being. Jerry allowed his head to fall against Philip's chest. Philip rested his chin on Jerry's head and closed his eyes, trying to imagine the pain that Jerry must be feeling. He rubbed Jerry's shoulders a little harder until the sobs began to subside.

"I guess I've been drunk for the past few years, haven't I?"

Philip didn't dare say a word. Not yet.

Jerry sat up a little. "What do doctors know, anyway?" He allowed a smirk to creep back onto his face. "This old girl's got a few years left in her."

Philip smiled into the mirror, and after giving just a couple more affirming rubs on Jerry's shoulder, he got up and leaned on the dresser so that he could look Jerry straight in the face.

"Nobody doubts your longevity, Jer. What concerns us—the doctor and your friends who love you—is that you don't take care of yourself. And I'm not going to make any judgmental statements here, but the fact is, Jerry, you drink too damn much. And this time—sure, you just fainted and needed to spend the night in the hospital to get re-hydrated or whatever it is they did to you. You were lucky, Jerry."

Jerry sat quietly during Philip's monologue, staring at his hands and the handkerchief that they held.

My hands look so old.

One last sniffle came, then he spoke.

"Okay, here's the deal. I know that I don't take care of myself, and I want to, if for no other reason than that I love you and my other friends. And I know that you want what is best for me. But…you have to be patient. Change takes time."

"Everything takes time, Jerry."

Jerry stood up, and this time the smile crossed his face with a bit more confidence. "Well, Mother's going to have to practice moderation, it seems. Let's get out of this bedroom before I make the moves on you."

Philip rolled his eyes and laughed. "I'll meet you out there in a couple minutes. Gotta go to the little girls' room."

Philip sighed as he relieved himself, thinking that their chat had not been so difficult after all. Then he heard a familiar sound coming from the kitchen, the telltale tinkle of ice cubes being dropped into a cocktail glass.

Philip closed his eyes and shook his head, muttering to himself, "I'm guessing today is not the day he begins moderation."

* * * *

It was a glorious autumn day, a perfect day to live in the French Quarter. Burgundy Street was quiet this early on a Saturday morning, and Philip was taking advantage of the stillness by strolling casually to the store and back. The walk to Matassa's Grocery was a mere five blocks or so, but he had taken a roundabout path there, walking down Burgundy to Cabrini Park, then circling the park and heading up Dauphine until he reached Matassa's. He didn't need to go shopping, but in the French Quarter, it's best to go shopping a little bit at a time, especially if transportation is limited to the two feet.

Now on his way home, Philip was wary when he turned the corner at Orleans and saw two men leaning in a doorway in the middle of the block. Instinctively, he walked out into the middle of the street and picked up the pace a little. He was fairly certain that the men meant no harm, but caution was something he didn't mind overdoing. As he passed the men, he glanced over and saw that they were homeless people who had probably been forced away from some other doorstep and had ended up together on this one. He felt bad about avoiding them, especially when it occurred to him that most ne'er-do-wells were out and about at night, rarely in the morning. He cocked his head pensively and made a mental note to dig out some of his old sociology books that dealt with crime and statistics. He'd have to refresh his memory on that subject.

As he drew near to his Burgundy Street home, a smile came to his face as the building came into view, and a feeling of warmth rushed through his body. He slowed his pace, wanting to savor this moment while it lasted.

He had never really had a boyfriend before. And though people often joked about his sordid past, hopping from one bed to another, his reputation far outdistanced his actual experience. The truth of it was that he had been looking to settle down for a long time, but whenever he met a man, the two of them would end up in the sack without much forethought about tomorrow or the day after that.

Philip sat down on the steps leading into his apartment. He wasn't quite ready to go in, at least not until he had finished reflecting.

He remembered that he had almost made the same mistake with Barry. But there was something about Barry that had made him keep his distance for a while. Barry had a sadness about him that sent a warning to Philip: "Keep away from this man if you have any sense of propriety."

That intuition had been correct. Barry had just gotten out of a relationship, and he certainly was not ready to get into another one. In other circumstances, Philip might have cast his ideals to the side and said, "Oh well, he doesn't want a commitment, but hell, he's cute, so I'm gonna do 'im."

As it turned out, Philip didn't "do 'im." And now he knew why. Almost from the moment they had met, he had been in love with Barry. He had never imagined it possible to be this happy. He rose from the steps, gathered the three plastic bags into one hand and opened the door with the other.

Barry was in the kitchen, making himself a cup of coffee. He gave Philip a big smile as he lugged the grocery bags onto the counter.

"You're becoming so domestic," Barry quipped. "What happened to the little tramp I met last year?"

Philip gasped. "If *that's* not the pot calling the kettle aubergine! You were the one who first put the moves on ME, remember?"

Barry had to smile. He loved getting Philip riled up like this. "I don't think so. I recall someone fitting your description throwing me down on the sofa and falling on top of me."

Philip looked puzzled. "So? That's not the FIRST move. The first move involves anything that is directly related to getting naked."

Barry grinned. Philip had his own way of creating his own theories about things. "Where in the hell did you get that idea? Anyway, you started it by rubbing my nipples, so I took off my shirt. Is that the first move?"

"Of course it is," Philip replied matter-of-factly. "You see, I didn't ask you to take your shirt off, so it was *your* move, not mine." Then he grinned and kissed Barry on the cheek. "I'm not complaining, by the way."

Barry was always fascinated by Philip's sense of logic. "You never fail to amuse me. You want some coffee?"

"Sure. I'll take another cup. I had one earlier, while you were still sleeping."

"You make it sound like I sleep in late every day," Barry said, "when in fact, I have to drag you out of bed every weekday morning."

"Okay, okay, enough about us already. What are we going to do about the kids?"

"Joel and Lance?"

There was no need for a response. Joel and Lance were the only "kids" they talked about.

Barry carried his coffee into the living room, with Philip trailing behind him with his own cup. They sat down and took a couple of sips before Barry spoke up.

"I think it's a lost cause. I don't think Lance is ever going to change. No, that's not true. But I don't think he's going to change for at least a couple of years, and I don't think that Joel should have to put up with his nonsense in the meantime. A few years is an eternity to someone twenty years old."

"Tell me about it," Philip answered. "Don't forget, I've got to listen to these students every day, and they like to make mountains out of mole hills."

They were still for a moment, sipping their coffee.

Philip dabbed at the corners of his mouth with his forefinger and thumb. "I have an idea, but I'm afraid you might not like it."

"Oh, God, here it comes." Barry threw himself back on the sofa with a defeated look.

"Cut it out," Philip said, reaching over and slapping him on the chest.

138

"Ouch!"

"You deserved that. Listen. They seem to trust us a great deal. I think we should have them over and open up a dialogue about it."

Barry furrowed his brows in disbelief.

"Yeah, right. And you think Lance is going to agree to that?"

"Well, if he doesn't, then at least Joel will know where he stands."

Another silence ensued as they stared at nothing and sipped coffee. Barry spoke up.

"I guess it wouldn't hurt, but I think they should do most of the talking. I feel a little funny, though. I mean, you listen to people's private lives every day during counseling. I might feel a little funny."

"Just promise them it's all private, so that they can trust us, okay? I'll call them in a few minutes."

* * * *

The four of them had decided to meet at Philip and Barry's house the next day, Sunday afternoon. Barry was going to barbecue after they had finished their "little talk."

Philip heard the door knock and almost yelled for Barry to get it, when he realized Barry was outside preparing the pit. He was up to his wrists in potato salad, but he had to answer the door. "Coming!"

He rinsed his hands and walked quickly to the door, flinging it open.

"Come on in, boys!"

But there was only one "boy" there, and he was crying.

Instinctively, Philip grabbed Joel by the shoulders and pulled him into an embrace.

"Oh, Joel. What's wrong? What happened?"

Joel sniffed into Philip's shoulder, crying as only a young person with a broken heart can cry. The sobs were only intermittent, but Philip could tell that he had been upset for some time.

Joel still had not answered Philip, though he had tried.

"Okay, Joel, it's okay. Come sit down here, and I'll get you something to drink."

Philip led Joel over to the couch, where he collapsed in a heap and covered his eyes with his hands.

"What would you like to drink, hon? I have coke, diet c-"

"Whiskey," interrupted Joel. "Straight up."

Philip blinked hard. "You sure?"

Joel pulled his face out of his hands and looked Philip in the face with his swollen, bloodshot eyes. "Yes. Bourbon, if you have it. Straight up."

Philip didn't argue and walked into the kitchen. Joel wasn't much of a drinker, and he wasn't sure this was a good idea. Under the circumstances, however, Philip was not going to question him.

The back door flew open and Barry walked in. "The kids here yet?" he asked, looking into the living room. As soon as he saw Joel, he knew something had gone awry, because as soon as Joel saw him, he replaced his face in his hands.

Philip tried to explain. "Uh, it's just going to be the three of us this evening, it seems."

Barry stared back and forth at the two of them.

"I don't know what happened," said Philip, reading the inquisitive look on Barry's face. "I guess we're going to find out in a moment."

Philip returned his attention to Joel, who was a bit calmer after the initial release of emotion.

"You have any Kleenex?"

Philip gave Barry a look, Barry nodded and headed for the bathroom.

"Barry's going to get you some, hon," said Philip, rubbing Joel lightly on the back and handing him a glass with two fingers of bourbon in it. Joel took a big gulp and grimaced.

Barry rushed back into the room and gave a box of tissue to Joel, who looked up at him with a wan smile.

"Thanks."

He paused for a moment while he blew his nose, then laughed softly.

"I guess that's kinda gross, huh?"

Philip smiled. "Only if you ask us to hold it for you. Here." He leaned over and grabbed the trashcan that was under the end table. "Just toss it in here."

Joel threw the tissue in the basket and grabbed another one to wipe his eyes. Barry took a seat opposite them, and he and Philip sat quietly, waiting for Joel to start talking.

Joel dabbed his eyes one last time, threw the tissue in the basket, grabbed the glass for another gulp, let out a great sigh and leaned back on the sofa.

"I don't know where to begin," he said.

"Why don't you tell us what happened today?" asked Philip. "What happened to make Lance not want to come?"

Joel paused for a moment, interrupting the silence with a little sniffle.

"Well, as you know, we all agreed yesterday that we were going to meet today with you," he said. "He did agree, but I don't know if you could tell, but he wasn't exactly crazy about the idea. Anyway, that was yesterday afternoon. Last night he started acting really weird, and…"

"What do you mean by 'weird?'" Philip interrupted.

"Like…like he was acting defensive about something. Like everything I said bothered him."

"Can you give me an example?" Philip asked.

Barry watched in silence, happy to see his counselor-lover at work.

Joel heaved another sigh. "Yeah. Lemme think…"

He looked up at the ceiling for a moment. "Okay, here's a perfect example," he said. "Okay, so we get this apartment together, right? It's already been about two months since we've lived there. So last night I asked him what we were going to do for the evening. It was a pretty innocent question, I thought. I ask him that just about every night. I wasn't sure if he had plans or not, so I just wanted to know so I could plan my own evening. No big deal, right? Wrong. He went off on me, telling me that he had his own life and that he could do whatever he wanted to. He said he wanted to do something with his 'normal' friends, since he had to do something with my 'queer' friends today."

Joel's eyes welled up with tears, and his face contorted with the pain that comes with uncontrollable emotion.

He held off the sobbing long enough to say, "I love him so much, but I guess he doesn't love me."

Philip and Barry exchanged glances. Nothing needed to be said. They were a lot older than Joel, to be sure, but they had each known the pain of a broken heart.

Philip drew a little closer to Joel and rubbed his back, and Joel fell against Philip's chest, where he resumed his crying.

With his face against Philip's chest, Joel sobbed, "Why can't he accept being gay like I have? If he loved me, he would."

"It's not that easy for some people, Joel," said Barry. "Especially if they're fairly certain that their family would reject them if they knew they were gay. I know. I used to be that way once."

Philip was all ears, but he tried to keep any obvious signs of his curiosity in check. Barry didn't bring up his past much, so this was a rare revelation.

"Some people need more time to deal with being gay," Barry continued. "Hell, I didn't admit it to myself until I was twenty-three. And even then, I didn't want to tell anyone. I was still dating women for a year after that."

While Barry talked, Joel quieted down a bit, but his face was still buried in Philip's shirt. When he realized that Barry was finished talking, he turned his head just enough to look at Barry and said, "Did you act like Lance is acting now?"

Barry thought for a moment and said, "Sadly enough, Joel, I think I did. And I'm really sorry for it now. But I speak from experience when I say that you can't force Lance to do anything that he doesn't want to do. Or isn't ready to do."

All was quiet for a moment, then Joel pushed himself up and said shyly, "Sorry if I got your shirt wet, Philip."

Philip smiled indulgently, "That's what shoulders—and shirts—are sometimes made for. It's okay."

Joel grabbed another tissue and honked again. This time, he didn't feel a need to apologize.

"That was last night. I guess y'all are wondering what happened today, huh?"

A tissue in the trash. Another tissue for his eyes.

"I stayed home last night and did some studying, and I went to bed before he got home. But he didn't sleep in. I heard the shower running about nine, and then half an hour later, he walks in all dressed up—a tie and everything. So I ask him where's he's going. 'Church,' he says. Lance never goes to church. Except when he's with his family and he has to. So I'm 'giving him his space' and all that crap…"

Philip winced a little. His social worker jargon had just been attacked.

142

"…so I didn't ask any questions. Then he comes back five hours later, barely in time to get ready to come here. When I tell him he'll have to hurry if we're going to make it in time, he got real nervous."

Joel was barely able to fight back the tears as he continued talking.

"So I asked him what was wrong, and he says that our relationship is unnatural and against what God intended and that we needed to…to change."

Barry and Philip exchanged glances again. Barry had to control himself, because he had a strong urge to roll his eyes. He had come from a fundamentalist background, so he could imagine what some holier-than-thou preacher had been telling Lance.

Joel had started to cry again.

"Rejection is one thing," he cried out, "but I can't compete with Jesus!"

* * * *

The sun was already behind the oak trees in Audubon Park, and long shadows had reached the bench where Lance had sat down after one lap around the park. He shivered as the early autumn chill crept under his sweatshirt and onto his damp skin.

He leaned forward, resting his elbows on his knees and letting his head hang. He looked at his sweatshirt upside down, and memories began to flood his mind. This was the same sweatshirt he wore to go to football practice when he was in high school. It was the sweatshirt he wore around the house to do chores. The same sweatshirt he wore while he was in his Jeep riding around town with his girlfriend. The same shirt he wore when Joel first kissed him…

Lance's eyes glazed over for a moment, and he shifted uncomfortably when he realized that he was getting an erection. What really made him uncomfortable was that the other memory—the one of his old girlfriend—had certainly not evoked that reaction.

* * * *

"Come on in!" Patricia hugged Sky and Steven as they came into her living room.

"I'm so glad you invited us over," said Sky. "It's been a while since just the four of us got together."

"It'll be nice to see Linda outside of the office," said Steven. "Where is she?"

Someone hollered from the kitchen. "SHE is in the kitchen cooking. Some things don't change. The only black person here is doing the work."

Patricia shook her head and rolled her eyes. "She can be so dramatic. I'd better get in there and help. Y'all can come on in and visit while we cook."

They walked into the kitchen to find Linda tying a bandana on top of her head.

"Nah, Miss Scarlet, you need to eat 'fo you go to a party."

Patricia rushed over and yanked the bandana off her head.

"That's awful! Don't do that! You're prolonging a stereotype!"

Linda laughed. "Girl, you white folks are too sensitive. It was a little joke. I can do it because I'm black and in a private home. You crackers, however, are NOT allowed to do this."

Patricia chuffed and started to walk away, but Linda grabbed her around the waist, swung her around and planted a kiss on her lips.

Patricia pretended to be annoyed, but you could tell she was happy.

"Well, I'll forgive you. However, I should point out that you were trying to do a Mammy reenactment, but you sounded more like Prissy, so you need to get your offensive *Gone with the Wind* stereotypes sorted out."

Patricia made cocktails, and they enjoyed some small talk while they finished cooking.

Linda clapped her hands. "Dinner is ready! Okay, boys, this will be contrary to Patricia's fancy uptown manners, but we are going to do this using the self-serve approach. Grab your plate off the dining room table and help yourselves."

Linda had a reputation of being a really good cook, so the "boys" wasted no time getting their plates.

"Linda, this smells so good," said Steven. "I've had your smothered green beans before, and I love 'em. Is this something you learned from your mother?"

She cocked her head. "Hmmm, let's see…Well, I learned from my mother to use a lot of butter and lard, so yes, I guess I did learn some secrets from her. I forgot to warn you that this is authentic soul food. That means it is good for the soul, but not necessarily for the body."

"I'll take soul over body any day," said Steven.

Thirty minutes later and sated, the boys said that everything had been delicious. Of course, they expected no less from "Chef Linda." Patricia announced that dessert was her responsibility.

"Don't be too impressed," she said. "I picked up dessert at Brocato's. You have a choice: spumoni or cannolis."

After Patricia had walked into the kitchen, Sky whispered, "Is she doing okay? I mean, it's been a few weeks since her dad died, but is she still depressed?"

Linda checked the kitchen door before she replied.

"She's getting better. There are still times when I find her crying, but not as often. She was really close to her dad. Sometimes I think she is taking it harder than her mom."

She glanced again toward the door to the kitchen. "Patti, do you need any help?"

"No thanks! It's going to take longer than I thought to get the spumoni out of the container. I'll be just a couple more minutes, I promise!"

Steven whispered, "Hey, I've been meaning to ask you something. Did you notice the woman in the back of church who was sobbing?"

"Wait, what woman? Was it a family member?"

"I don't think so," said Steven. "She was in the last pew on the side aisle. She came in late and left early."

"Do you remember what she looked like?"

"We couldn't tell," said Sky. "She was wearing a veil that completely covered her face. I'm talking about the kind of veil that you'd see in an old Italian movie. Possibly two veils. She definitely did not want to be recognized. I looked for her again at the cemetery, but she wasn't there. She left right after communion, so I guess she wanted to slip out before anyone tried talking to her."

"Interesting," said Linda.

"Seriously, this woman cried almost the entire time she was there," said Steven. "Whoever she was, she was really broken up. I kept thinking that only someone in love would cry like that."

Sky swatted his arm. "Hush! We don't know that. Let's not talk about it now."

Linda saw movement at the kitchen door, so she cleared her throat. "Need help carrying it in, hon?"

Patricia walked in carrying a rather large serving tray. "No thanks. I managed to get it all on one tray. What was all that whispering going on in here about?"

There was a short but awkward silence.

Patricia laughed. "It's okay. I know a lot of people are concerned about me, but I promise I'm doing much better."

She put the tray down on the sideboard with a loud clank.

Linda stood up. "Good lord, woman, what is all that you brought in here?"

Patricia raised her arms in glee.

"Surprise! Everyone gets *both* desserts!"

* * * *

Jerry was sweating.

He looked at his watch for the umpteenth time that hour, counting away the minutes before Barry and Philip were coming over. He passed by the bar as he walked into the living room. It took a great deal of will power for him to keep himself from stopping. He couldn't even look in the direction of the bar. It was like a dirty picture—if he looked at it, it might get him excited long enough to commit some moral sin.

He stopped. He turned back around, heading in the direction whence he had come.

He stopped again, swearing.

"Damn! I just want to have a little drink! Is that so much to ask?"

He felt the blood rush to his head as the anger came and went.

He had been thinking all afternoon about how he was going to deal with the visit from his two tenants. He had already heard the lectures from Philip about his drinking problem.

"I don't have a drinking problem," he mumbled to himself. But then a coldness crept into his bones, a certain chill he felt when truth inevitably asserted itself. The truth had always been there, like a lion that he had managed to evade for a long time. Jerry was tired of running. He was cornered. It was time to turn and look the beast in the face.

Jerry dropped into his chair, which began to rock slowly, then slower, until it was completely still, and so was he.

So maybe I do have a little drinking problem.

He knew it. But what was the big deal? He was in his sixties. He wasn't hurting anyone. Except maybe himself.

"You're hurting yourself," Philip had said.

So? So what? Who cared?

In his head, he could hear Philip's voice saying, "I care."

Jerry tried to muster the energy to get out of his chair, but nothing happened. He thought of the bar, then he looked at his watch. Twenty more minutes until they arrived. He sat perfectly still, like a cicada preparing for a seven-year hibernation.

I won't have a drink until they get here. Then they'll see I don't have a problem.

* * * *

Jeffrey

There was a good vibe at The Pub tonight. DaShawn, Philip, and Barry had gone out for dinner, and they decided to pop in for an after-dinner drink. They lucked out with a table, because it was standing room only. And loud.

Philip leaned toward them and yelled, "It's almost ten. I guess some of the twinks got here a little early so they can get stamped for upstairs before they have to pay for it."

DaShawn grinned at him. "Hey, as I recall, when you and I met here a few years ago, we would come early to save a few bucks."

Barry said, "Don't flatter him. It was more than a few years ago."

Philip gave Barry a shocked look. "I'll always be younger than you. Besides, we were penniless graduate students at the time, as I recall."

While the three of them were talking, DaShawn had been throwing occasional glances at a handsome man who was standing just inside the door looking very uncomfortable. He was almost six feet tall with warm, caramel skin and close-cropped, tight, curly hair. He was well dressed, but it looked like he was dressed for a social event rather than a night of clubbing. He had a nice build, and the couple of extra inches in his girth looked good on him. He looked over at DaShawn, and they locked eyes for a second.

Probably another closet case, thought DaShawn. He had become an expert at picking them out the past few years.

I hope he practices safe sex.

He refocused his attention to his companions for a few minutes before standing up.

"Ok, boys, I'm going to call it a night."

Philip groaned. "It's so early! When did you get old?"

DaShawn laughed. "Hey, I have the early shift at Lazarus tomorrow. You don't come until *late* morning, remember?"

"Actually, I'm kind of tired," said Barry. "I went straight to dinner from work, remember?"

Philip gave him a pleading look. "Please, pretty please, just one more drink!" He grabbed Barry's arm and pouted.

Barry pretended to be exasperated. "Okay, okay! But just one more drink."

Philip turned to DaShawn and winked in triumph. "So…are you heading to Rampart Street for some illicit activity?"

"No, not tonight." He winked back. "I had a great time, though. Thanks, guys. I'll see y'all soon, I hope. And you," he added, pointing at Philip, "you had better be on time tomorrow morning!"

He glanced one last time at the door to look at the man, but he was no longer there. He gave them each a hug and slipped out of one of the side doors. He had only taken a few steps when someone behind him touched his arm.

"Excuse me."

When DaShawn turned, his heart caught in his throat. He found himself face to face with his sexy mystery man. Maybe the chemistry was only for a second or two, but it was enough for DaShawn's heart to quicken. Then he noticed that there was something different about the way the man was looking at him.

It looks like he's afraid.

DaShawn wasn't quite sure how much time had passed, but he managed to clear his throat and find his voice. "Yes, can I help you?"

The man seemed puzzled by the question. "No, I…I don't need any help. I'm not a tourist or anything like that." He looked up and down street before looking back at DaShawn. "I noticed you in the bar. I was wondering if…if we could talk."

"Well, uh…I was just heading home, but…what is it you'd like to talk about?"

He was looking up and down the street again.

"Is it okay if we get off the street? Maybe get a drink?"

DaShawn didn't know for sure where this was going, but he already had a suspicion.

"I guess we could go back in-"

"Not there!" The man seemed a little embarrassed by his interruption. He looked at the ground for a second. "Sorry, I didn't mean to cut you off. I was thinking maybe some other place. I like the Blacksmith Shop, if that's okay."

It was less than two blocks away, and also the direction he was heading, so DaShawn decided to go with it. The guy didn't seem dangerous, and the bar he suggested was a safe, public place—a public straight place, he noted.

"Sure that's fine."

They resumed walking in that direction.

"By the way, my name is DaShawn." He extended his hand.

The man looked abashed as he shook his hand. A little spark went through DaShawn's arm.

"I'm Jeffrey. Sorry, I guess it was impolite of me not to introduce myself upfront."

DaShawn realized that his heart was beating faster. He dismissed it, attributing the quickening to what could have been a dangerous encounter with a stranger. He tried to relax.

"Nice to meet you, Jeffrey. I don't think I've seen you around. Are you new in town?"

"Oh, no, I grew up here. Seventh Ward. I just don't go out much."

Once again, he looked away. DaShawn was uncertain of what—or how much—the guy wanted to say next.

"But I'll tell you more after we get settled." He opened the door for DaShawn, and they went in. Jeffrey ordered the drinks and insisted on paying for them.

"Hey, it's only fair. You're doing me a favor, remember?"

The bar wasn't too crowded, so they were able to find a table just far enough from the hubbub.

DaShawn raised his glass. "Cheers."

Jeffrey smiled. "Cheers." It was the first time he looked relaxed since they met. DaShawn's heart jumped again.

Stop reacting like a 16-year-old.

"So what is it that you want to talk about?"

"Well…" Jeffrey fidgeted with the cocktail straw for a bit before looking back up with an awkward smile. "I think you've probably figured out by now that I'm kind of new to this."

DaShawn was glad he was getting right to the point. He allowed himself to smile, but it was hard not to laugh out loud.

"Yes, I think that's pretty obvious. Exactly how 'new' are you?"

"Very." He looked down at the straw for a second. "That was my first time in a gay bar."

"Wow." DaShawn wasn't completely surprised, but this admission allowed him to use his psych theoretical background to take into account what the guy was going through emotionally. "It's a big night for you, I guess."

"Yes, you could say that."

"May I ask why you chose me?"

He shrugged his shoulders. "You seemed kinda normal. And there were only a few black guys in there, and I wanted to talk to someone who could relate to my situation."

DaShawn nodded. "Okay, I have decided that you're not a serial killer, so we can talk for a bit."

Jeffrey chuckled. "Thanks, I guess."

DaShawn leaned closer to him. "Well, maybe you could start by telling me what your 'situation' is."

For the next twenty minutes, Jeffrey did most of the talking. His family owned a retail store, which he managed. He was now separated from his wife, and he had joint custody of their two children. The oldest was a boy who was going to be a high school senior, and his daughter was a freshman.

He asked DeShawn to talk about himself, which he did, but soon DaShawn moved on to the next topic.

"Now I'd like to know a little personal information. You haven't even mentioned being gay yet."

Jeffrey looked shocked that DaShawn just said "the g word" out loud. He glanced around him to see if anyone else had heard him.

"I, uh…I guess I'm not really comfortable talking about these things in public."

Part of DaShawn wanted to laugh, but he knew what Jeffrey was going through, because he had gone through it himself. "I'm sorry if I said it too loud, but I can assure you that—with all the noise around us, nobody can hear us. It's okay if we talk about it. I'll be sure to keep my voice down.

Jeffrey relaxed a little. "I guess that's okay. Where should I start?"

"Maybe you could start when you first thought you were gay, then tell me about your experiences with men."

Jeffrey took a couple of breaths before continuing. Once he got started, the words began to flow unhindered. Most of what he said didn't surprise DaShawn. He had feelings for boys back in junior high, then realized he was sneaking more than a few glances at naked athletes in his high school locker room. Then he'd had a few experiences with men in college, mostly drunken sex. He got married right after college, and it wasn't until about a year ago that he met a man—a customer—and had a tumultuous three-month relationship.

He shook his head, looking defeated. "I was so naïve. I honestly thought that this guy was in love with me. I was already imagining spending the rest of my life with him, only to find out that he was a player. By then, the damage had been done. I told my wife I wanted a separation and, of course, I had to tell her why. She threatened to tell the children."

Those last words got caught in Jeffrey's throat, and DaShawn looked on with compassion as he struggled to swallow his pain. Almost a minute later, he cleared his throat and continued.

"Anyway, that's the gist of it, I guess. Only my wife knows. Now I'm in limbo, trying to hide my feelings from the rest of my family while trying to experience more of this other side of me that I barely know."

DaShawn prompted him with a few question, and Jeffrey began to relax again, spilling his heart out onto the table between them. As his spiel began to wind down, he looked DaShawn in the eyes and smiled.

"There was another reason why I chose you. You were—by far—the sexiest man in the bar."

He stretched his leg under the table, and DaShawn's heart began to beat faster when he felt a shoe-less foot rubbing his inner calf.

"Thanks for hanging out with me. I'd like to get to know you better." His foot traveled a little higher to DaShawn's inner thigh. "Is your place nearby?"

* * * *

Yet again, Joel was feeling exhausted by his confrontation with Lance. He didn't think he would be able to handle much more of this constant bickering.

"Do you want me to move?"

Joel's question was what Lance had been waiting for. But now that the time had come, he wasn't so sure about his answer. He paused for a second, looking into his mind for the prepared script. It had become fuzzy.

"I think that might be best. It's obvious that you have no intention of trying to pursue a normal life, and…"

"My life *is* normal," blurted out Joel, the color rising to his cheeks. "Maybe not for you, but for me, it's perfectly fine."

Lance felt his own anger growing. "That's exactly my point! You live in this little fantasy world with all these other gay guys. Don't you know that there are a whole lot of other people out there? Most of the world is not like you, Joel. Don't you understand that?"

Joel felt the tightness in his throat. He was afraid that his next words would crack, showing Lance how frail he felt, how much he loved him. He swallowed hard and gathered his strength.

"I understand a lot more than you think. One thing I do understand is that you're lying to yourself if you think…"

"I'm NOT lying! Lying is living the way that you live. You're lying to *yourself* if you think that you can live a normal life being the way that you are."

"Is that what this is about? Living a normal life? What are you afraid of, Lance? Are you afraid of not having Daddy's money? Of not having respect? Friends? What?"

Lance turned away from Joel, but not soon enough to keep Joel from seeing a brief flash of pain in his eyes.

"Leave my family out of this. There's no way we…there's no way *you* can live being gay. I mean, how do you expect to live? How do you expect to make money? Or get a job?"

Joel softened a little. He was angry and hurt, but now he saw the real Lance shining through the tough exterior, which was showing a few cracks.

"We—or anyone else—can be gay and live just fine. Just think of the people that you've met. Philip, Barry, Steven, Sky. What about Patricia and Dorothy? They all have jobs…"

"Yeah, right," Lance cut in, snorting with a caustic laugh. "Sky comes from money. So does Patricia. And do you think that Philip and everybody else really makes that much money? I want to be successful, Joel. I don't want to live with a bunch of queers in a ghetto. I want a nice house, a nice car, a nice job…I can't get that living with you."

Joel's face fell, and Lance knew that he had said something horrible, but he went on the defensive even more, rising from his chair in a huff and walking toward the kitchen. He refused to soften his position.

This is the way that a REAL man acts. Strong and silent. Like my dad…

It took a moment for Joel to find his voice. "Nice house? Nice car? What about a nice wife? You didn't say anything about that! Did you have any particular woman in mind?"

Lance spun around and yelled back, "You know what I mean, Joel! Don't say anymore. It's not about you, it's about living with *any* gay man, not just you."

Lance disappeared into the kitchen and rummaged around in the refrigerator for a Diet Coke. His heart was pounding, and his legs were wobbly. He knew that he was wrong about some of the things that he was saying, but he felt trapped. He felt like there was no escape from the hell that Joel had created for him. Joel was too close, and he needed space.

Joel followed Lance into the kitchen and stood a few feet away from him. Lance remained standing with his back toward him.

"I'll need at least a few days to move out," Joel said quietly. "It'll take me some time to find a place to live."

Lance took a swig of his Coke and paused for a moment. Refusing to turn around, he said, "Thanksgiving isn't that far away. When we…when I come back after Thanksgiving, try to have everything gone, okay?"

Joel's eyes welled up with tears.

He doesn't even love me enough to look at me.

Not wanting to risk Joel seeing the hurt on his face, Lance didn't turn around as he headed for the back door.

If only he knew how I really felt.

"Lance?" Lance stopped at the door, his hand frozen on the knob.

Joel went on, weakly, "If I start dating…women…again…could I stay here?"

Lance cocked his head in surprise. "We can talk about it."

A minute later, Joel was staring at a closed door, trying to decide if insanity was a reasonable price to pay for love.

* * * *

Barry and Philip were lounging on the couch, enjoying their post-repast stupor.

"It was great hanging out with DaShawn tonight," said Barry. "I'd like to spend more time with him, if he wants to."

Philip put his feet in Barry's lap. "I'm pretty sure he enjoys hanging out with us. The issue is more about his being able to find time. Sometimes his job keeps him well into the evening hours."

He wiggled his toes. "Please rub my feet?"

Barry pretended to be bothered, but he enjoyed rubbing Philip's feet.

"I forgot to ask you," he said. "Yesterday, did you see the way that Jerry's hands were shaking? Before he had that drink?"

Philip shook his head sadly and walked off.

"Where are you going? I barely rubbed your feet."

"Brush my teeth. If you want to talk, come here."

Barry followed him into the john.

"Yes, hon, I noticed. But he's an adult, and there's nothing I can do about it. Right now I'm more worried about Joel than about Jerry."

Barry reached for his own toothbrush. "Did he call today?"

"No. I'm concerned about him."

"As soon as you finish brushing your teeth, call him, okay? Otherwise you'll be fidgety all night."

* * * *

Joel was so near the telephone that the ringing scared him. He looked at the caller ID and saw that it was Philip. His immediate urge was to answer, but he knew that he couldn't. He rubbed his hands together, nervously.

I have to let them go if I want to keep Lance.

The machine beeped, and Philip's cheery voice filled the room. "Hi, Joel and Lance, this is Philip. Joel, give us a call, even if it's late. We wanted to see how everything was going. You know the number. Bye."

Joel waited until he heard the dial tone on the answering machine before he picked up the receiver and dialed.

"Hi, is this Wendy? It's me, Joel…yeah, I know, I kinda disappeared. How's everything…good…hey, how about catching a movie with me?"

* * * *

DaShawn was still unlocking the door when Jeffrey started to undress him. They tumbled forward together into the narrow side gallery, shedding clothes and groping each other.

A heavy workload had been depriving DaShawn of sex, and he was hungry for it. He grabbed Jeffrey's head and leaned in for a passionate kiss. Jeffrey moaned in response and began tugging on DaShawn's belt buckle.

"I want you so bad," said Jeffrey, shucking the last of his clothes onto the floor.

DaShawn shoved him backwards onto the bed and crawled on top. Jeffrey wrapped his legs around his waist.

"You are so fuckin' sexy," said DaShawn. "I gotta have you."

He opened the drawer to his nightstand and pulled out a condom.

Jeffrey hesitated for a second, but then he gazed into DaShawn's eyes with a pleading look. "I…I want you to."

DaShawn took his time, slowly getting Jeffrey to relax. When the moment came, DaShawn raised himself on his arms so that he could look into Jeffrey's eyes and gauge his reaction. His first push evoked a gasp from Jeffrey.

"Easy, take it slow."

"Okay, baby." DaShawn saw Jeffrey's eyes widen; a moment later, he heard him moan in surrender.

* * * *

156

Wendy

Lance's Jeep bounced its way down St. Charles Avenue.

"It's freezing," cried Wendy from the back seat, snuggling against Joel to keep from shivering.

Instinctively, Joel put his arm around Wendy, though he was doing it to be chivalrous, not romantic. "Even with the top on, this thing is like a refrigerator," he said.

Lance sat stiffly in the front seat, glancing occasionally in the rear-view mirror to see how Joel was handling himself. He noticed Joel's arm around Wendy, so he felt compelled to reach over and place his hand on top of Jena's.

Jena turned to him. "You'll have to do more than that to keep me warm," she said with a flirtatious smile.

Lance grinned mischievously, giving her hand a hard squeeze before returning it to the wheel.

"So we all agree on Tip's, right?" He asked the question while looking once again in the rear-view mirror.

Everybody murmured approval, and Lance turned onto Napoleon Avenue. He was thinking of reaching over to hold Jena's hand, but he stopped when he noticed that she was already doing something with it. Up it went to her very-blonde hair, where it found a place behind her ear before it swept the hair behind her shoulder. Her motion caused her perfume to stir, and he caught a whiff of it.

It sure is funny how men's and women's perfumes are so different, he thought. His mind raced back to a long-ago memory of a steamy sex scene on the couch with Joel. He closed his eyes and gripped the wheel tightly, trying to clear his mind.

"You all right?" asked Jena.

Joel perked up in the back seat. "What's the matter?"

"I'm fine," said Lance, embarrassed. "What do you mean?" He tried to affect a puzzled simper, hoping to cover the fact that he was flustered.

"It's no big deal," said Jena, rubbing his cheek with her hand, "but you were driving with your eyes closed for a couple of seconds. That's not exactly a normal thing you do when you drive, is it?"

Lance just stared ahead, not knowing what to say.

Joel could tell his friend was embarrassed, so he came to his aid, as he often did when Lance found himself in awkward social situations.

"Well," Joel said, "his driving couldn't be much worse, could it?"

All four of them laughed, grateful that a difficult moment had passed.

Seconds later, Lance spotted a parking spot less than a block from Tipitina's. He pulled in quickly. "God, are we lucky, or what? I must be livin' right."

Joel's chest tightened at those words. What did he mean by "living right?"

Was that directed at me? Is living right being straight? Or at least acting it?

The four of them tumbled out of the Jeep and made their way toward the club, two by two.

Joel felt odd with his arm around a woman. Even though he and Lance had never publicly displayed their affection—not that Joel didn't want to—Joel had become more accustomed to moving his hands along the hard lines of Lance's body, not the soft curves of a woman's.

Two by two, thought Joel.

I guess Noah wouldn't have had any room on his ark for ME, would he?

He glanced up at the sky, as though his question were a prayer.

When he looked back down, he saw that Lance and Jena were holding hands. Déjà vu, he thought, his eyes riveted on the back of Lance's head.

This is going to be a long night.

* * * *

PJ's Coffee was quiet, but far from empty. Students were scattered everywhere with books sprawled on the tables before them. Of course, not all of them were studying; in fact, probably less than half of them were, but the other half had taken on that "cram for final exam" whisper mode. Wendy was in that mode, while Joel was trying desperately to study.

Joel took a sip of his Granita and tried to concentrate on his history textbook.

Wendy wasn't even trying. She had been attempting to engage Joel in conversation for at least fifteen minutes, but all she was getting in return were grunts and head nods. Finally, she snapped.

"Joel, how can you study that shit?"

Joel put down his book and glared at her in frustration. "Wendy! You're driving me crazy! I've been screwing around for the past month, so I've really got to study!"

Wendy took a sip from her latté and looked at Joel reflectively. Joel thought he had gotten through to her, so he went back to his studying. It wasn't going to be that easy, it turned out.

Wendy piped up again. "Are you and Lance still fighting?"

Joel's heart began thumping, but he pretended not to be bothered by her question. Without looking up, he asked, "Whaddya mean?"

Another pause as Wendy sipped on her coffee.

"C'mon, Joel. The two of you are always being nasty to each other."

Joel squirmed around in his seat. *What does she mean*, he thought.

"You know how it is. We've just been friends for so long that we sometimes act like…like…"

Wendy smirked. "Like lovers?"

Joel looked up. His heart was now pounding so hard that his ears were ringing. His voice was barely audible to himself as he said, "Something like that."

Wendy laughed softly, then took another sip. She had managed to get Joel's full attention, and she was taking advantage of it.

"So when are y'all gonna make up?"

Joel was in a panic now. Not so much for himself, but for how this was going to affect his relationship with Lance.

"What are you talking about?"

"C'mon, Joel. It's so obvious that the two of you are in love. By the way, if he wants to pretend, why is he dating that girl, anyway? She's a tramp."

Joel was having difficulty keeping his mouth from hanging open. He was utterly disoriented by this turn of conversation.

I've gotta think quickly.

He blurted out, "She seems okay to me. Lance seems to like her. What would you think if somebody said that about you?"

Wendy nodded her head from side to side as she continued to grip her cup in both hands.

"It's not the same thing," she said. "You and I aren't dating."

"Whaddya mean, we're not dating?"

Wendy looked at him in disbelief. "Joel, I enjoy being with you, because you're a great guy. But we're not really dating, because you're gay."

She said it so matter-of-factly that Joel was taken by surprise. In fact, he was so surprised that he forgot he was supposed to deny it.

"You…you know that? I mean…why would…how…?"

Wendy put her cup down and leaned over the table, apparently incredulous at his bumbling.

"Duh! Joel! Snap out of it, man! Doesn't everybody know? I mean, I've seen you dancing at The Parade, and I've seen you hanging out a lot with that counselor…what's his name, and everybody knows he's gay."

"But lots of straight people dance at The Parade…" Joel's attempt at denial just faded away when he could tell Wendy was not going to be fooled by anything he said. His heart began to beat a little slower.

"Does it bother you? That, you know, I'm…you know…"

"Of course not, silly. Like I said, I think you're a great guy." She paused and added, "I'm not sure if I feel the same way about Lance, though. He seems like a jerk sometimes."

"You can say that again."

"Have y'all been together since you were freshmen?"

Joel felt so relieved that he could answer candidly. "Me and Lance? Unh unh. We were just roommates until our sophomore year. Then…well, things just sorta happened."

Wendy smiled into her cup and raised her eyebrows. "I'd love to hear the details."

Joel was shocked. "Wendy!" He started to laugh, and he couldn't conceal the blush on his cheeks. "I can't believe you said that!"

She just giggled even more. "Joel, I'm not the saint you make me out to be. I may seem that way to you since we've never done anything, but that's only because I knew you were gay after we had gone on a couple dates last year."

"Really?" Joel was intrigued. "How did you know?"

Wendy rolled her eyes. "Joel, I just knew. For one thing, you're practically the only guy who's taken me out that didn't try to get me in bed the first night."

Joel couldn't believe what he was hearing. "My GOD! You knew all that time?"

Suddenly, he felt so much lighter. He didn't realize the burden of lying until it had been lifted. He found himself smiling at Wendy.

He asked, playfully, "So…are you trying to tell me that you're a whore?"

Wendy assumed a smug, sophisticated expression as she lifted her cup to her lips.

"Not a whore, Joel. Just a woman of the '90s."

* * * *

DaShawn was still patting himself on the back. It was Friday night, and on most Fridays he would be lounging at home, eating leftovers in front of the TV. Tonight was different because he had a date. Tonight he was on his way to a restaurant to meet Jeffrey. A week had passed since they hooked up, and DaShawn was atwitter about seeing him again.

It was their first real date, so he wanted to impress the guy. DaShawn had suggested Dooky Chase's for dinner, but his date said something about going there last week, so he wanted to try another place. Before he could make another suggestion, Jeffrey suggested a sushi restaurant. Somewhat surprised, DaShawn agreed and offered to pick him up. He had only eaten sushi a few times, and that was with his white friends. Only one of his black friends, Jerome, had agreed to try it out with him, but he said that would be his last time to try "some of that crazy food."

When he walked into the restaurant, the place was almost empty, so it was easy to spot Jeffrey in the back corner, though he was facing away from the door.

He walked up behind him and squeezed a shoulder before taking a seat next to him.

"Did they seat you all the way back here?"

"I asked them to," he answered. "I figured that we could have more privacy this way."

DaShawn sensed that something else was going on by the way Jeffrey looked down and began to rearrange the cutlery. Then again, he had only met the guy once before, and maybe this was the way he acted in a restaurant.

They had just enough time to exchange pleasantries when the waiter arrived with their menus. Jeffrey opened his right away, and DaShawn was amused by the way that he was so focused.

Jeffrey sighed, put down the menu and chuckled.

"Okay, I don't know much about sushi, okay?"

DaShawn grinned at him. "Well, we are probably in the same boat. I've only tried it three, maybe four times, so I won't be of much help."

They decided to get two sushi rolls that they decided were "safe" for neophytes—the California and Philadelphia rolls—plus the Dragan roll to be a bit more adventurous.

When there was a lull in the conversation, DaShawn decided it was time for him to do what he needed to do.

"Jeffrey, there's something I need to talk to you about."

As soon as the words were out of his mouth, Jeffrey froze and stared at him.

"Okay." DaShawn looked frightened.

162

"That wasn't a good way to start, I'm sorry. It's nothing bad."

Jeffrey relaxed and gave him a small grin. "Okay, that's good."

"I feel that I need to be honest about something," DaShawn continued. "For some time now, I have had a rule that I don't date men who are in the closet."

Jeffrey went back to being tense. "But I told my wife…"

DaShawn nodded. "Yes, that's the most important step, but you haven't told your family and friends."

Jeffrey looked like he was both angry and ashamed at the same time.

"Wait, hear me out," said DaShawn. "Don't worry, I'm not giving you an ultimatum or anything like that. I mean, it's only our first date."

Jeffrey smiled and relaxed again. "You're not counting the time we met?"

DaShawn was relieved that the tension had lessened. He smiled back.

"I don't think that counts. We went from a bar to my bed. Don't get me wrong, it was some of the hottest sex of my life."

"Glad to hear that I measure up." Jeffrey used his foot to give a quick nudge under the table.

DaShawn knew that he needed to stay on task, because if he didn't, he would lose his nerve.

"Look, I just need to say this. I have had some bad experiences with guys in the closet. Getting stood up, never answering or responding to calls, that sort of thing. I decided to bend my rules just a little because I felt like we had a real connection."

"The feeling is mutual." Jeffrey rubbed his leg under the table again.

DaShawn laughed and moved his leg away. "Cut it out! I'm almost finished. I am willing to see where this goes without getting serious. I think you could really use someone to talk to, and I am willing to be that person. At least for a while."

It was obvious that Jeffrey was grateful.

"You've been great, DaShawn. I really do appreciate your understanding and all that, but…you do know that I want to do more than just talk, right?"

"As a matter of fact, I do know that." DaShawn had a mischievous grin. "I'd like to do more than just talk, as well. In fact, I'd like it a *lot*. So can we do dinner again next week?"

Jeffrey's smile faded. "I'm not sure. I think it might be difficult to see each other so close to Thanksgiving and all that."

DaShawn was puzzled. "You have time off from work, right?"

"Oh sure," answered Jeffrey. "We're closed Thursday, and we have other employees who'll be working the weekend, but I want to spend as much time as I can with my children and my parents."

"Well, of course you should." DaShawn was a little embarrassed that he hadn't thought about that. "Family is important. I'll be spending time with my family too. What about the weekend? You think maybe you can get away Saturday afternoon and Sunday? I was thinking we could go hiking and maybe even camp out for a night."

Jeffrey grunted and looked away, like he was trying to think of what to say. He mumbled something about having the kids that weekend.

"Did I say anything wrong?" DaShawn leaned closer to him. "You seem to be bothered by something."

Jeffrey sighed and looked at the table for a few seconds, then he sat up and looked directly at DaShawn.

"Look, I made plans with my wife and kids already, okay?"

DaShawn felt his heart sink.

I can't believe I've been duped again by a married man.

"Look," Jeffrey continued, "my wife and I are legally separated, but I haven't found a place on my own yet, so I still live with them. I guess I…I should have told you that."

DaShawn could feel his ire building. "Yes, Jeffrey. Maybe you should have told me, because that seems to be a pretty major sticking point, don't you think?"

DaShawn wasn't new to this. The pieces started to fit together. He shook his head angrily.

"Now I get it. I'm so stupid. You picked this restaurant because none of your friends or family would ever come here to eat. Am I right?"

Jeffrey's eyes registered surprise.

"Oh yes," DaShawn continued, "I know exactly how this game is played. Well, I don't play that game anymore. I'm done being used by guys like you." He stood up, threw some bills on the table, and started for the door. "Nice knowing you."

* * * *

The high-pitched beeping of the telephone intercom startled Philip. He reached for the receiver.

"Yea, Carol, what's up?"

"There's someone here to see you, Philip."

Philip closed his eyes in exasperation. "Carol, I really need to get some work done. I don't have any appointments. Who is it?"

"It's Joel."

Philip bolted upright in his chair. "Omigod. Carol, you're so good! He's probably the only person I would let interrupt my schedule right now."

"Uh, yes sir, I'll tell him you'll be out in a second."

"Carol, is he alone?"

"Uh…well…uh…*no*, you don't have any appointments for at least thirty minutes. I'll tell him to have a seat."

"Who's with him?"

Apparently, Carol had grown weary of the game of giving disguised answers, because she hung up.

Who is with him? Philip thought. *Is it Lance? I don't know if I can handle this right now.*

Duty forced Philip out of his chair and into the short hallway that led to the receptionist's office. The other person was a young woman whom Philip did not recognize.

Joel beamed from ear to ear when he saw Philip, who came forward with his right hand out. Joel ignored the hand and threw his arms around Philip's neck.

"I've really missed you, Philip. I'm sorry that I haven't called you in a while."

Philip remained professionally cool. "We can talk about that in a little while. In the meantime, you might want to introduce me to your friend here."

Joel laughed. "I'm sorry. My manners get worse by the day. Wendy, this is my friend Philip. Philip, this is my girlfriend Wendy."

* * * *

Jack

Lance wasn't aware of the fact that he was staring until the man began to walk in his direction. When he realized that the guy was headed straight for him, Lance panicked. Getting up from the park bench, he tried to make a getaway, but it was too late.

"Don't I know you from somewhere?"

Lance froze, then turned to face the man. He quickly surveyed what he had been staring at moments before: a gorgeous man, almost six feet tall, with black hair and deep brown eyes. Lance was a sucker for brown eyes.

"I don't think so. Maybe."

The hunk gave Lance a smile, then said, "I thought from the way that you were looking at me that you knew me."

Lance shifted from foot to foot. "Oh no, it's just that...you reminded me of someone. You could be his brother."

"Who is that?" the man asked.

Lance's eyes bulged and he just stood there, speechless. The man laughed.

"I see," he said with a casual gentleness. "I was just going to walk around the park a couple of times. You wanna join me?"

"Sure," said Lance, relieved that he wasn't going to be beaten up.

"My name's Jack."

"I'm Lance. Nice to meet you."

Lance wasn't even frightened by this stranger. What did scare him was that he was already thinking about doing more than just walking in the park.

* * * *

Even before they had gone halfway around Audubon Park, Lance was totally at ease with this handsome stranger and happy about the prospect of getting to know him a little better. For some reason, his scruples had been tossed to the wind as soon as this guy had walked toward him just twenty minutes earlier.

"So…let me guess," said Jack. "You're a business major, right?"

Lance grinned. "That's pretty good. How'd you guess?"

"Just intuition. And a little logic. For one thing, you haven't tried to move our conversation into some philosophical realm, so I pretty much ruled out liberal arts."

Suddenly, Jack stopped walking, and Lance naturally stopped as well and turned to face him. Brazenly, Jack's eyes moved up and down Lance's body as a mischievous smile crept onto his face.

"You know, you're built enough to be a jock, but for some reason I figured otherwise."

Lance backed away a little and fumbled for a response. "Whaddya mean? I mean, I work out…and I used to play football in high school…"

Jack let out a deep, masculine, throaty laugh. It was obvious that he was delighting in Lance's nervousness.

"I have a feeling that you're *usually* the calm, cool and collected type," Jack said as he resumed his walking.

Lance followed in step. "That's what I've been told."

"Then why are you so nervous around me?"

Lance walked along quietly for a while, his head down. He was searching for an answer that wouldn't make him look like a fool. *I really like this guy*, he thought, *but I can't believe I'm acting like a teenage girl after the way I've acted toward Joel.*

"Lance, there's no reason to be nervous. I…I like you, even though I just met you."

Lance turned to him and smiled, unconsciously picking up his pace as he did so.

"Thanks. Me too," said Lance. "I don't know if I've ever had an older friend before." *Shit! I probably insulted him.*

Once again, Jack let out that throaty laugh.

God, that's sexy, thought Lance. *And those brown eyes. And his shoulders…*

Jack asked, "Do I seem that old to you?"

Lance tried to cover his embarrassment by smiling back, saying, "Of course not. That's not what I meant."

"Yeah, right," said Jack with a chuckle. He stopped again and looked at Lance, who walked two or three more paces before turning around.

"How old do you think I am?"

Lance pursed his lips and thought for a moment. "I dunno…twenty-eight?"

Jack beamed and said, "Don't bullshit me, man. You know I'm older than that."

"No, really," said Lance. "I can't tell."

Jack reached over to grab Lance's shoulder, which he shook good-naturedly. "Flattery will get you everywhere, believe me. I'm thirty-five."

His hand remained on Lance's shoulder just a second longer than necessary, and Lance's heart began to pound. Jack's face took on a serious look, then he glanced all around him, as if he were looking for someone, though no one was nearby.

"Do you mind if we make a pit stop?" he asked. "It's right over here."

"No problem," said Lance. "I could use a little relief myself."

At those words, Jack looked quickly at Lance, surprised, then as he turned to walk toward the public toilet, he smiled to himself. *This kid has no idea what he's saying*, he thought. *God, how I love the innocent ones.*

The two of them walked to the urinals, and just as Lance started to pee, he froze as he felt a hand go down the back of his sweat pants.

* * * *

"Does your friend mind waiting for you out there?" asked Philip, who was closing the door behind him while Joel took a seat on the couch opposite his chair.

"Nah. I won't be long. I just wanted to talk to you for a little while. In fact, Wendy's the one who talked me into coming."

"Really?"

"Yeah."

Philip grew quiet. His experience as a counselor told him to sit still and let Joel do the talking.

Joel's face took on a more serious look before he went on.

"Philip, I'm really sorry about the way that I acted toward you. You didn't deserve that. But let me finish before you say anything, okay?"

"Okay."

"Basically, what happened was that Lance gave me an ultimatum. I had to move out if I wasn't going to try to be…you know, straight. Or, like *he* said, 'normal.' Anyway, I love him so much that I was afraid to death to be away from him. I can't explain it. It's like I couldn't imagine life without him. So I decided to go along with his insanity and start dating again. Wendy's the girl that I was dating last year. Before I came out, remember?"

"I don't know if you ever mentioned her name, but yes, I do remember your talking about dating someone."

"Good. Well, she's really been cool, and the reason why I liked dating her was that she never put pressure on me to…you know, to do stuff."

Philip smiled. "I think I get your drift."

"Good," said Joel, smiling in return. "Well, today I found out WHY she never pushed me to do anything." Joel paused for dramatic effect, then practically yelled, "She told me that she figured out I was gay the first time that she met me!"

Philip was having difficulty refraining from laughing out loud. "And how does this tie in to your visit here today?"

Joel calmed his exuberance and said, "It's like there's been a huge part of me that has been locked up these past few weeks. For some reason, just hearing Wendy say that she liked me even though she knew I was gay…just hearing that made me feel so happy. It's hard to explain."

"Sometimes we need affirmation from other people," said Philip, trying to keep Joel talking.

"But it's more than just that," Joel said. "Basically, she told me that Lance was an asshole and that I deserved a whole lot better than him. I think I'm going to leave him."

Joel looked as though he was not going to continue, so Philip thought it was okay for him to finally throw something in. "You know, Joel, decisions like this should be made after careful thought…"

"You don't want me to move out?" Joel interrupted. "I thought you wanted me to break up with him."

"I never said that," said Philip.

"Then why are you trying to talk me out of it?"

"I'm not trying to say that either," said Philip. Joel was looking confused and was prepared to blurt out something else, so Philip went on, "Let me explain, Joel. This has to be your decision, and your decision alone. The reason why I'm suggesting careful thought is so that you won't regret this decision later."

Joel looked reflective. "Okay, I see your point. You're right, as usual," said Joel, smiling.

"Well, of course I am." Philip smiled in return. "I'm good, huh?"

* * * *

"Can we get together again some time?" Lance asked.

Jack was peeking out of the door as he tucked in his shirt. He looked at Lance in surprise. "You want to…uh…are you sure?"

"Of course I'm sure," said Lance, immediately regretting what he had just done with this man. "Don't you…want to see me again?"

Jack looked nervous and pleased at the same time. "Yeah, I guess. I mean, of course I do. It'd be nice to see you again." He looked out the door one more time. Without turning back to Lance, he said, "Hey, wait at least a half minute or so before coming out, okay? You can catch up with me. I'll be back on the track, walking."

He headed outside, leaving Lance standing there, confused. A minute or so later, Lance caught up to him.

Jack turned to him and smiled, then quietly asked, "You want to meet here again tomorrow?"

Lance turned to him and frowned. "Here? In the park? I was thinking of maybe getting together for a cup of coffee. Or maybe you could have me over for dinner, something like that."

Jack looked at the ground and unconsciously began walking faster. Lance matched his pace, his mind racing. I'm such an idiot, he thought. *I guess it's a bit soon to ask a guy to invite me over to his house for dinner.*

When a few seconds had passed without a response from Jack, Lance tried a different, humorous tack. He smiled at Jack and playfully punched him on the shoulder.

"So, I guess this means you can't cook. Darn, and I was looking forward to a home-cooked dinner."

"That might be kind of hard," replied Jack, who was looking more than a bit uneasy.

"Whaddya mean?" asked Lance. He wasn't accustomed to rejection. "What's the big deal about a dinner?"

There was a long pause before Jack said, "I don't think my wife would understand."

* * * *

It was a clear, crisp winter day, beautiful in so many ways. Usually, on a day like this DaShawn would be smiling, maybe taking an early evening walk with friends, laughing and swapping family stories from the holiday weekend.

But not today.

Today he was feeling dejected and frustrated, and the longer he listened to Jeffrey's justifications, the more agitated he became.

"Listen to me," Jeffrey pleaded. "You don't know what it's like having children. It's a lot of responsibility. Part of that responsibility involves knowing what to say—and what *not* to say—to your children."

DaShawn could feel the vitriol churning within him.

"Oh, I think I understand, so are your parents children? I guess not, so why haven't you told them?"

Jeffrey was clearly not prepared for this new line of attack. He fidgeted, buying time for him to try to get the upper hand again.

"You also don't know what it's like to work in the real world. In the real world, when you manage a business that is owned by your family, you have to keep things to yourself to protect the business relationship you have with your other family members."

DaShawn's anger erupted. "That's a load of crap, and you know it! Remember, I *do* work in the real world, and if you don't think counseling drug addicts day after day is real, then you'll need to explain reality to me. Believe me, it's about as real as it gets."

Jeffrey opened his mouth to say something, but DaShawn stopped him with a raised hand.

"I'm not finished! Also, in the 'real world,' most people don't have the luxury of guaranteed employment after college. Most people have to work their asses off just to get a goddam interview, and then another one, and then another one. And you know what else? Try getting those interviews when you're black. Maybe that's what you're really afraid of. Maybe you're afraid that—for the first time in your life—you will be on your own."

Jeffrey was seething with anger. His inner voice was telling him that he didn't have to take this crap, but that last comment stirred the part of him that was silent, protected, shoved in a corner, hidden in a place he didn't want to look. When he looked back up at DaShawn, he was still angry, but it was anger mixed with a child's fear of being rejected and alone. Of being cut off. He stood up so fast that he knocked his chair backwards onto the floor.

"Damn it! I don't think dating someone is supposed to be this difficult, so obviously this is not working."

He picked up the fallen chair then headed for the door. Before he got there, DaShawn had something else to add.

"I guess that confirms my final suspicion. You're not serious about a relationship. If you're walking out the door now, you're saving me a lot of trouble down the road. I'm glad I know now not to waste any more time on you!"

Jeffrey probably didn't hear the last word, because he had already slammed the door behind him.

* * * *

Joel was absent-mindedly flipping through a magazine, bored out of his mind. Indian Hill didn't feel like home anymore. After living in New Orleans for over two years, Joel felt like a stranger in his little hometown in the suburbs of Cincinnati.

He smiled to himself as he recalled a quote from Tennessee Williams: "America has only three cities: New York, San Francisco, and New Orleans. Everywhere else is Cleveland."

"Joel, you want something, honey?"

He looked up to see his mother beaming down on him. She was wearing an apron over a perfectly ironed, pleated red dress. He could tell she had taken great care to put on her makeup and do her hair, even though she was not going to see anyone but immediate family on Christmas Day. If she had been wearing pearls, she would have been a dead-on match for Mrs. Cleaver.

"No thanks, mom. I'm fine."

"What's so funny?"

"What?"

"You looked like you were trying to keep from laughing." She gave a little gasp and touched the corners of her mouth. "Do I have something on my face?"

"No, mom, you're fine." This time he did laugh. "Sorry, but I was just thinking about how Lance sometimes refers to you as Mrs. Cleaver."

She pretended to be perturbed, but she was smiling, with a hint of a blush.

"That boy," she said. "He should come visit soon. Is he getting along better with his dad?"

"Pretty much the same, I guess."

Joel thought it might be a great idea if he and Lance could switch fathers for a little while. Lance's dad was always extolling Joel's virtues as a dedicated student. Lance said that once his dad made a crack about trading him in for a "Joel."

Joel's parents wouldn't trade him for the world, but he knew that his dad had been disappointed that he wasn't more athletic. He could see the gleam in his dad's eye when he was talking to Lance about sports. Lance's dad wanted him to be more studious, but Joel's dad would have been much happier if his son spent a little more time on the field and less in the library.

He had put tremendous pressure on Joel back in high school. He had appeased his dad somewhat by joining the track team. In fact, he had excelled, doing quite well in cross-country events. Joel had briefly considered trying wrestling—his dad's favorite sport when he was in high school—but when he watched a match and saw how tight the uniforms were and how much body contact there was, there was no way he was going to put himself in that situation. No, he thought track was definitely a safer bet because it was easier to hide a boner in loose running shorts. Plus, he could often avoid the locker room by telling the coach he was going to jog home after practice.

His mom's relationship with Lance was even more baffling. When he came to visit, Lance felt quite at ease with Joel's mom, often cajoling her and sometimes even flirting with her. His mom ate it up. Sometimes Joel got a little jealous when they so easily transitioned from their banter to more serious topics. In many ways, Joel's mom treated Lance like a peer.

Joel couldn't say anything about his relationship with Lance's parents because he barely knew them. An obvious inequity existed, namely that Joel had only been to Lance's house once, whereas Lance had been up to visit him in Ohio at least four times. What really bothered Joel was that it would be so easy for him to visit Lance. Joel drove home for the major breaks between semesters—December and the summer—and it would be relatively easy for him to make a detour to go through Memphis, where Lance's parents lived.

Joel felt a familiar ache. He had learned to ignore it, for the most part, but every now and then something gnawed at his guts. Lance didn't love him as much as he did. Or maybe Lance was just ashamed of him. He wasn't sure which was worse.

His mother smiled and reached down to caress his hair.

"It's always so nice having you back at home."

Joel hadn't told them anything about his strained relationship with Lance. How could he? His parents didn't know they had a "relationship" to begin with. How could he talk to them about going back to dating girls when they didn't even know that he had stopped?

She went back toward the kitchen, leaving Joel to resume his reverie.

He missed Lance so much when they were apart. Even now, he wanted to call him constantly, just to hear his voice. His dad had complained last year when the telephone bill had come in. This year, he was trying a new tack. Before leaving at the end of the semester, he told Lance he had worked out a way to send a "signal" to him. Joel would call Lance's house, let it ring once, and hang up. That was the sign for Lance to call him back. Lance's parents didn't mind the phone bill. They credited Joel for keeping Lance's academic head above water.

Still, Joel wasn't satisfied because he didn't get to talk to Lance as much as he wanted. Less than half the time, when Joel would try the "one-ring" method, Lance would call him back. He'd say something like, "Joel, you're being paranoid. I wasn't here, so how could I hear the phone ring?"

But why doesn't he want to talk to me as much as I talk to him? Why doesn't he just call me on his own?

Joel admitted he was being a little insecure; even so, he had reasonable doubts about those times when it appeared to him that Lance was avoiding him. He recalled a somewhat heated conversation the two of them had before parting ways for the holiday.

"I think you're ashamed of me or something. Why can't I come visit you after Christmas? On my way back to school?"

"I don't want my parents to get suspicious."

"Why don't you just tell them?"

"Tell them what?"

"Duh! Just tell them that you're gay and get it over with."

"I'm not gay!" Then Lance had gone silent for a few seconds as he glared at Joel. "They can't ever know. I told you that was a condition of our being together…as friends. If you can't live with that, then it's over."

The memory was fresh, and the pain in Joel's chest was just as real now as it was when Lance told him that over a week ago. Each time he thought of it, the knife pierced his heart.

He can be so cruel sometimes.

He knew that Lance's stubborn state of denial sometimes made him unkind, but Joel held on to the hope that Lance would come to his senses again—that they would be more than just roommates pretending to be straight. Every time Joel got angry enough to think about just breaking it off with him, other memories would creep back in. He would recall Lance's touch, the hard curves of Lance's body, the first time Lance had surrendered himself to him, moaning with pleasure…

Joel rearranged the magazine on his lap.

He realized his hypocrisy was blatant. After all, he hadn't told his own parents yet. And why hadn't he? Right now was a perfect opportunity. His older sisters and their families weren't here yet, so it was just the three of them for at least another couple of hours.

I wonder…

He looked over at his dad, reading the newspaper through the bottom of his bifocals, his pipe next to him on the light stand. Joel noticed his dad was just beginning to show small signs of aging: new wrinkles, a little less hair, and a slight stoop when he walked. He was fifty-seven years old, which wasn't exactly ancient, but most of his friends' fathers were still in their forties. Joel had been kind of an "accident." His two sisters were in junior high school when he happened along.

His mom called out to them from the kitchen, "Would one of you please put the music back on?"

Joel had been so engrossed in thought, he didn't notice that the music had stopped.

"Sure, mom." Joel knew that when his dad was reading the paper, he was oblivious to anything being said, so it was up to him to take care of it. He spotted the remote on the other side of his dad's chair.

"Hey, dad."

His father didn't respond, so Joel hollered, "DAD!"

The paper rattled as his father turned to him, surprised.

"Mom wants some music. Look, the CD remote is right next to you."

"Oh, yeah, sure," he murmured. He fumbled with the remote, alternating between looking through the top half and bottom half of his glasses.

Joel was always amused by his dad's discomfort with technology.

"Just hit 'Play', dad. It's that big button with an arrow, the one right in the center."

His father grinned a bit as he aimed the remote at the console.

"Smartass," he said.

Joel chuckled. He knew his dad didn't really mind the ribbing. A second later, the music resumed, and Bing Crosby's silky, sonorous voice came through the speakers.

Joel sat back and took in his surroundings. He was living in a picture-perfect setting so quintessential that it bordered on comical. The air was filled with the aroma of freshly baked pies and honey-baked ham. Bing was singing "White Christmas," and Joel's mother was humming along with him. His dad was re-lighting his pipe, and the tree lights blinked red and green a few feet from a crackling fireplace. It was a postcard Christmas except for one thing: the young man in the picture was gay.

Just then, to make the scene look even more like a cover of the Saturday Evening Post, his mom walked up and handed his dad a fresh cup of coffee.

"Here you are, Bill. That other cup must be cold as ice by now."

His dad grunted, the standard accepted combination of acknowledgment and gratitude. He barely looked away from the paper.

"Thank you."

Wow, thought Joel, he took the time to thank her. Must be the spirit of the season.

"You're welcome, dear," she said. "Joel, you sure I can't get you something?"

"No thanks, mom."

Why haven't I come out to them yet?

He trusted them, and he had no doubt that—no matter what—they would always love him. Maybe it was time.

His mother started back to the kitchen.

"Hey, mom, hold on…"

She turned to look at him, smiling expectantly.

"There's something I've been needing to tell you both."

"Yes, dear?"

She's so happy. What if I ruin her day by telling her something like this?

He glanced over at his dad, who had crumpled the paper in his lap and was looking back at him.

"Is anything the matter, son?"

"Oh, no, dad," he started. "I…"

Maybe coming out to your parents on Christmas Day isn't such a good idea…

He cleared his throat. "I just wanted to tell you both how much I appreciate all that you've done for me."

His mother walked back toward him, performing her signatory hair-stroking gesture. His dad had already begun rearranging the paper, though Joel was impressed that he had taken the time to swivel his chair a little to look back at him head-on. That was something.

"We're very proud of you, son," he said, swiveling back into his reading position.

His mom bent at the waist, giving him a kiss on the cheek. A minute later, his dad was back to reading the paper and his mom was placing another pie in the oven. The postcard remained perfectly intact.

* * * *

Lance lay in bed, utterly still. He glanced over at his alarm clock—just after midnight.

He was back at his parents' home in Tennessee, and from where he lay he could see the bleak, early January sky through both his window and the skylight above his bed. He felt so alone looking up at all of that blackness.

"Why can't I just be normal?" he said softly to himself.

He had been thinking of Jack. Why was he suddenly so into a married man he had met in Audubon Park? Lance didn't know why, but he was a little obsessed with Jack. He knew that he loved Joel, but there was something about Jack that made him irresistible. Was it because Jack was older? Stronger? Taller? Unattainable? Maybe it was because Lance was accustomed to people falling for him, and Jack seemed almost disinterested.

And sex in a public place…that was hot.

Lance recalled what transpired between them, and he grew aroused with an intensity that he had never before known. He tossed about, trying to ignore his urges and focus on what he had been hearing from his counselor at the Church: "When you feel these unnatural urges, just pray to Our Lord and ask Him to take them away from you," or "If you must, imagine your future bride in a wedding gown and reflect upon the beauty of procreation when love is shared between a man and a woman."

Despite his mood, Lance had to smile. I guess it worked, he thought. *That whole bridal gown thing makes me limp pretty quick.*

Lance usually ended up fantasizing about the groomsmen, not the bride.

A thought occurred to him, and as it did so, his heart began to thump with excited anticipation. Could he do it? Would he? Would he dare do something so risky in a town where many people knew his father?

The urges in him grew so strong that he could no longer control himself.

His mind made up, and his body even more determined to find the release that his mind could not satisfy, Lance threw on some clothes and quickly groomed himself He looked at himself in the mirror from right to left, admiring the way that his blond hair had grown longer and how his unblemished, masculine face was handsome and defined. Satisfied with his looks, he tiptoed down the stairs and out the back door, making his way to the garage, where his Jeep was waiting. Normally, he would have dreaded climbing into his Jeep in this kind of weather, but since his mother had talked his father into having the garage heated, the interior of the car was only slightly cool.

He turned the key and felt a surge of power and control as the Jeep roared to life.

"To hell with what people think," he said to himself. "If I want to cruise the park, it's my business and no one else's."

* * * *

Barry reached for the phone, but his eyes never left the report on his desk.

"Barry speaking. Can I help you?"

"That depends," came a sultry voice. "What can you do for me?"

"That depends on who you are," said Barry, getting a little nervous. He didn't recognize the voice on the other end of the line. It certainly wasn't Philip.

"Who is this?" he asked after a moment's silence. There was a snicker on the other end, one that he immediately recognized.

"Dammit, Joel! I thought some freak had gotten my number."

"I guess you were right," said Joel. "I am kind of a freak."

"Weird maybe. Eccentric, definitely, but not freaky. How've you been? Philip told me you had come back into the fold."

"I didn't realize that I had strayed," said Joel, "but I guess you can say I spent a little time in another pasture. Oh, and the grass was definitely NOT greener on that side."

Barry assumed a serious tone. "We were really worried about you. You know, I'd love to get together with you and do a little catching up. I can't really get any information out of Philip. You know how he is about confidentiality and all that crap."

"I guess that's a good thing," said Joel, "so don't go hard on him. I haven't been out very long, but long enough to know that you shouldn't entrust any secrets to just any queen. Maybe that's why they don't want us in the CIA. It has nothing to do with blackmail."

"For Chrissakes, Joel, get off it. When are you going to come over? And will there be a duo coming or will you be coming solo?"

"Can we get together for dinner and drinks this week? And it'll be a duo. My friend Wendy would like to meet y'all."

"Wendy?"

"You don't remember, but I'm sure I told you. She's the girl…"

"Oh, I remember," said Barry. "She's the one you used to date. Does she know…"

"Yes, she knows," interrupted Joel. "And we've become better friends. Hell, she said she knew pretty much knew I was gay the first time that we went out. I wish she had told me then. It would've saved me a lot of angst."

"Well, bring her along. Can't wait to meet her. Is tomorrow night okay?"

"Cool! I have another two weeks off before the semester begins, and Sky really doesn't need to keep me late at the store now that the Christmas rush is over."

"I'll ask Philip to be on the safe side. Let's plan for 6 p.m. How's that?"

"Perfect. I can't wait to see y'all again! You're the gayest friends that I have."

There was complete silence on both ends of the line.

"Uh…that didn't come out right," Joel was stumbling over an explanation. "What I meant was…"

Barry's laughter interrupted him. "I know what you meant, but can you do me a favor? When you come over, I want you to say the exact same thing to Philip."

* * * *

Jeffrey spoke with a penitent tone in his voice. "I really missed you this week. It made me realize a lot of things about myself, and…about you."

DaShawn was moved, but he reined in his emotions. He wasn't a novice at this sort of thing; he could tell that Jeffrey was looking for a chip in his armor, and he was intent on not letting it show.

"So," Jeffrey continued, "do you think we could come to some sort of a compromise?"

DaShawn was hoping to hear that word: compromise. He was hoping to achieve this small gain, because he knew it was a big step for Jeffrey.

"What sort of compromise?"

Jeffrey looked at the neighboring houses. "Could I please come in?"

"Afraid of being seen on a porch talking with a gay man?"

Jeffrey's face fell. "That's not fair. We're talking about a serious subject, but you're making me feel like I'm trying to sell you a set of encyclopedias."

DaShawn tried to suppress a smile but failed.

"Okay, come on in."

He poured two glasses of water, and they sat at the kitchen table.

Jeffrey took a long sip. "Thanks, I was thirsty. So, please hear me out. I want to propose a compromise. I was thinking that you and I could come up with a series of steps that I need to take to…to satisfy you.

DaShawn sighed. "I think it's sweet that you want to appease me, but it's not about me. These are things that you need to do for yourself, things to make your life better."

Jeffrey looked down at his hands. "Okay, I understand that, but…"

DaShawn held his breath waiting for him to continue.

"…But I feel lost. I feel lost without you. I need someone to help me through this."

DaShawn couldn't help himself. He reached over and passionately kissed Jeffrey, who seemed a little surprised—pleased, but surprised.

DaShawn sat back in his chair and tried to compose himself.

"I guess I need to be honest too. I have really missed you."

Jeffrey smiled and reached for his hand. "Can we talk about the steps I need to take?"

DaShawn returned the smile. "Of course we can. And if you have time after that—and only after—maybe you can 'step' into my bedroom."

* * * *

Despite the patches of snow on the ground, Lance could feel the sweat building in his armpits as he tugged at the steering wheel to make a U-turn. He had seen a couple of guys parked along the side of the road, and one had caught his eye: a man in his thirties, parked in a BMW. After he made the U-turn, he was surprised to find the parking spot empty. As he passed the spot, however, he saw some headlights come on under a nearby oak tree.

The car pulled up behind him and kept pace with him. Not sure what to do at this point, since this was his first time, Lance drove for a while to see if the guy would follow him. He did. A minute later, his heart pounding so hard and fast that the blood in his head was nearly blinding him, Lance pulled over to the side of the road. The car behind him did the same.

There was a moment of silence when the world seemed to stand still. Then the quiet and darkness was shattered as another light came out of the darkness—a flashing red light. Then he heard the dreaded words from a loudspeaker…

"Please step out of the vehicle."

In Lance's terrified mind, the flashing red lights were blinding beacons from the gates of Hell, and the voice from the loudspeaker came from the devil himself.

Lance's hands froze on the steering wheel. The cold January night just got a lot colder.

"Omigod, Omigod," Lance kept repeating to himself.

What am I gonna say? What am I gonna tell him?

The "him" was his father. Lance hadn't considered the possibility of fearing the officer.

The loudspeaker sounded once again, this time a little louder and a lot less friendly.

"I said, step out of the vehicle."

Lance quickly got out of the car, trying to look self-possessed. He walked to the back of his car and fumbled in his back pocket for his license. He felt awkward with the lights glaring at him and no one else in sight. He heard the policeman calling out his license plate number into a radio, and shortly afterward he heard his own name being called out in response by an incredibly bored woman whose voice was muffled and barely intelligible.

"One ticket…twenty years of age…"

Lance waited for another minute before he heard movement in the car and saw a figure moving toward him. He was a surly-looking yet handsome policeman: Thirtyish, five foot ten, broad shouldered.

Lance's observations were disrupted when a flashlight was pointed at his face.

"Can I see your license, please?"

The officer's eyes found Lance's and stayed there even after he had received the license from him. Lance found the look unnerving and turned to look at the ground, acting as humble as he could. After a few seconds the policeman broke his gaze to look at the plastic card with his flashlight.

"Officer, was I speeding or…?"

In reply, the policeman looked up and curled his lip in a snarl. He returned his gaze to the license then back up at Lance.

"You know, this is public property, but it's not legal to loiter here. Especially after 10 p.m."

Lance's fear began to subside a bit. He decided not to let this man know that he was the least bit afraid of him. After all, he was somebody in this town, wasn't he? Well, his father was.

"Officer, I was just driving through. I couldn't sleep, and I was just out for a drive to kill some time." He managed a hint of a smile.

The officer wasn't going for it. "You been drinkin', boy?"

Lance chuckled, "No sir, not me. Not tonight. The last thing I had before I went to bed was a cup of coffee."

A strange look came over the officer's face. "Coffee, huh? I guess now you know why you can't sleep."

Lance chuckled again. "I guess you're right." He was trying his damnedest to get chummy with the guy.

The look on the man's face turned hard again. "You Henry's boy?"

Lance tensed. "Yeah. You know my dad?"

"I know him well enough to know that he wouldn't want to see you driving around this park in the middle of the night."

He let his words sink in before going on.

"You know what they do out here, son?" Lance was getting awfully nervous, but he tried to go along with the dumb act. He shrugged his shoulders and shook his head a little.

"I didn't see anything going on, officer. I just saw a few other cars driving around. I figured maybe they were having a problem sleeping too."

He chuckled, but the man's face remained cold and still as marble. Lance cleared his throat to cover his nervousness.

The officer turned his head and spit on the ground. "You used to play halfback, huh?"

This is good, thought Lance. "Yessir. You a Cougars fan?"

"Sure am. Used to play running back myself. Made all state my senior year. About ten years back, so I guess you wouldn't remember."

The silence grew again. Lance was starting to like the guy a little, even though he seemed a bit "slow."

"Officer, uh, Cougar to Cougar, are you gonna charge me for anything? Cuz man, my Dad gets pissed if I jay walk. Know what I mean?"

The policeman's stare was unnerving, so much so that Lance began to shuffle his feet back and forth, gazing down at them from time to time to avoid the man's eyes.

Lance could take the torture no more, so he blurted out, "Could you let me off with a warning?"

The policeman's stony gaze transformed slowly into wanton glances as his eyes traveled up and down Lance's body. A grin formed somewhere on his face as he said, "Boy, you know the only people who hang out here this late are queers."

Lance's heart began pounding. "Whaddya mean? Not...I was just..."

"What d'you think your Daddy would say if I told him you was hangin' out around here?"

Lance's breathing picked up pace. He didn't know what to say to get out of this without somehow giving himself away.

"Aw, man, Officer...you don't think..." Lance's words trailed off.

The policeman looked all around him, as though he were making sure that he was alone, then he turned back to Lance and spoke in a low, deep voice.

"I tell you what, son," he said as he adjusted his crotch, "why don't you come on over and sit in the front seat of the cruiser there."

The man's smile turned into a leer. "I think I know somethin' you can do that'll make me forget all about this evening."

* * * *

Twelfth Night was one of Jerry's favorite holidays. Like so many festivities in New Orleans culture, it was a holiday that marked the end of one season and the beginning of another. The Christmas season becomes part of the past, and on this day, people in South Louisiana turn to the next season of mirth and merriment.

For most Americans, the sixth of January is just another day. For those Christians who follow the liturgical calendar, it is the feast of the Epiphany. In the Western tradition, this day recalls the theophany and the subsequent arrival of the Magi, or the "three kings." In New Orleans, it is so much more than that. Of course, there is a nod of recognition given to the Christian holiday that is made manifest by the sudden, abundant availability of king cakes stuffed with little baby

Jesuses. Even this tradition, however, has overflowed its original date and spilled into the following weeks.

For people in New Orleans—people like Jerry—January 6 is the beginning of the Carnival season. Mardi Gras dates change from year to year, but Twelfth Night is always on the sixth day of January. And on this night Jerry decided to throw a party with a little help from his friends.

"Philip, chop faster!"

Philip groaned. "I'm not good at this. I usually buy my seasonings pre-chopped."

"You're a disgrace." Jerry turned to yell into his living room. "Anyone else want to volunteer? It seems Philip does not possess elementary cooking skills."

Heads turned his way, laughter followed.

Linda squeezed Jerry's arm. "I'll help you, hon."

Jerry raised his hands in the air. "Hallelujah! Philip, you're fired."

Philip threw a dishrag at Jerry. "I'm just warning you, Linda, this man is a tyrant in the kitchen."

Jerry threw the rag back at him. "Hush, child. Leave the adults alone so we can cook." He patted Linda on the cheek. "Merci beaucoup, cher."

She smiled. "De rien. Happy to help. What is my assignment?"

"Just finish cutting up the seasonings there and let them simmer. Everything else is ready. It's a last-minute addition: mini stuffed bell peppers."

Philip walked out of the kitchen looking glum. Barry motioned to him.

"Come sit next to me, hon."

Philip plopped down on the loveseat. "Oh, that man! He's so demanding in the kitchen! He makes me feel like I'm incompetent."

Barry smiled and put his arm around him, and Philip's body automatically molded itself right into his. At that moment, Barry experienced his own epiphany.

We fit.

Yes, this is what he felt like when he was with Philip: He felt like they "fit" together. The best parts of his day were the ones spent with Philip. Snuggling on the couch watching TV, the morning coffee ritual,

186

the sweet chats they had in the dark before dozing off. He mussed Philip's hair and leaned in to whisper in his ear.

"First of all, I assure you that you're definitely *not* incompetent in the kitchen, but more importantly, you're an extraordinary expert in the bedroom."

Philip laughed and kissed him on the lips. He felt a little charge that made his spine tingle.

He's so amazing.

Philip had never dated anyone this long. He thought for sure that Barry would have tired of him by now. Then again, his problem in the past was that he was the one who got bored with whomever he was dating and started looking for a new beau after a couple of months.

Not this time, thought Philip.

I can see myself waking up next to this man for the rest of my life.

Darlene shouted, "Anyone else want a cocktail? Somehow, I got suckered into bartending again, but I will try not to take it out on you."

Quite a few hands went up.

"Lord. Okay, well Jerry is pushing the champagne, so let's start with that."

"I'll help," said DaShawn. "You do cocktails, and I'll pass around the bubbly."

"Thank you so much! Jerry had better feed them soon. They're getting rambunctious. Weren't you supposed to bring a date?"

"Oh, uh…" DaShawn was hoping he could avoid that question tonight. "His work got in the way. Maybe the next party."

He was anxious to change the subject.

"Hand me that bottle, if you would, and I'll get started, okay?"

Jerry was hollering from the kitchen.

"Dinner is almost ready, but first we are going to have some appetizers. Mini stuffed peppers! Just a few more minutes."

There was a chorus of complaints.

"Oh, be quiet," said Jerry. "I have been dragging my tits across this stove for hours, so get a grip! If you're starving, put a little extra fruit in your drink."

Linda banged the wooden spoon on the pot one last time.

"All done, Jerry. I waited until just now to add the parsley. Oh, and I hope you don't mind that I put in a little basil too. I think all you need to do is mix in the rice. You need anything else?"

Jerry beamed at her. "Basil, of course! Thank you for that! Darlin', you have been a godsend. The peppers are already soft, so all I need to do is spoon the mix into them and grate some cheese. Thank you so much! I think I can take it from here."

"Okay, holler if you need me. In the meantime…" She raised her voice. "Where's my wench?"

Patricia had been chatting with Sky and Steven, but she stopped when she heard Linda's voice.

"I'm over here, wench!"

Steven stood to give Linda a hug. "Thank god you're here. I can't get these two to stop talking shop. If I hear one more tragic tale about trying to make a living on Magazine Street, I'm going to pull out my hair."

"Oh puh-lease," said Sky. "You two are always swapping gossip about that nasty law firm y'all work for."

Patricia chimed in. "Okay, let's make a deal. No more shop talk tonight!"

Linda sat next to her and kissed her on the cheek. "Amen to that!"

Even now, Patricia blushed like a schoolgirl when Linda kissed her in public.

She's so out of my league, thought Patricia. Every time they walked into a room, people stared and stopped talking when they saw how beautiful Linda was.

"Are you blushing?" Linda laughed. "One of the many reasons I love you so much."

She's so out of my league, thought Linda. People stop talking and gawk at her every time we enter a room.

Jerry started tapping his cocktail glass with a fork.

"Quiet, everyone! I have something to say."

"No surprise there," said Philip.

"You'd better be quiet. Barry, put a sock in his mouth. So, let's see…Oh! First, I want to point out something obvious. If you look around, you will notice that most of you are half my age."

"More like a third," quipped Philip.

Jerry wagged his finger at him. "Be nice. Only one boy is less than a third of my age, and it's that little angel Joel over there."

"Thanks Jerry! For the record, I can also be a devil."

"Bless your sweet little heart. Are you legal yet?"

Darlene giggled. "Run, Joel, run!"

"Ha, ha, yes, I know that I have a reputation for being a chicken hawk, even though I haven't raided the chicken coop for quite some time, but the truth is that I enjoy being with younger people. I mean, I did invite some of my contemporaries, but they have become doddering old men."

Philip cleared his throat. "And this from a doddering old man!"

"Barry, could you please keep him under control? Children are to be seen and not heard. Where was I?"

Darlene prompted him. "Something about inviting some old people."

"Thank you, Darlene, you're now my favorite tenant. So yes, I invited a few of them and they had excuses about not wanting to be out late and all that nonsense. Still, I love them and always will, but you are with me now. Mother and her chickadees! Now that I have given you a little bit of an explanation about why I am so blessed with being surrounded by such lovely young people, I would like to make a toast. Get your glasses ready. DaShawn, would you mind passing that bubbly around again? Thank you. So…where was I? Oh yes, so most of you here were quite young in the early '80s, so you were spared much of the loss many of us felt when AIDS took so many of our friends. I was lucky, because I had Gary all those years and for many years before that, but when he died a few years ago…"

Jerry choked up. He squinched his eyes and held his hand over his mouth while he regained his composure.

"Just a moment. Mother will be fine."

While the room held its breath, Philip sidled up to Jerry and put his arm around him.

"Take your time, Jerry."

Jerry took a deep breath. "I'm okay, precious. Thank you. Grab a tissue for me, dear, would you? I want to finish this toast, but I guess I'd better make it quick. I would like to toast my dear friends who have gone before me, and I would like to toast all of you who are here now and who have made my heart complete again. So, raise your glasses…Here's to friends old and new!"

A round of "cheers" went up from everyone.

Philip handed Jerry some tissue. "You okay, Jer?"

"Of course I'm okay! Mother just got a little weepy, that's all."

Barry stood up. "And here's to my favorite landlord and dear friend, Jerry!"

"Here, here!"

Jerry walked over to Barry and put his arms around him.

"Thank you, my sweet boy. If ever you get tired of Philip, just let me know. You can move in here."

Philip moved in to make Jerry the middle of a hug sandwich.

"No such luck, Jerry. He's stuck with me."

"That makes me happy, precious. Now let me go. Mother needs to powder her nose. Oh, I almost forgot."

He yelled, "Mini peppers fresh from the oven! Help yourselves!"

He made for the bedroom, but as he reached the hallway, he turned around to take in the scene before him. His heart filled with joy.

Such wonderful, blessed young people. I'm so lucky to call them my friends.

He dabbed his nose with the tissue, sighed, and smiled.

Thank god for my friends, my family.

The End

About the Author

Kyle Scafide is an author and public speaker who lives in New Orleans. He received a B.A. from St. Joseph Seminary College and began graduate studies at KUL in Belgium. He finished his M.A. at Notre Dame Theological and earned his Ph.D. at the University of New Orleans.

For several years, Dr. Scafide was editor-in-chief of *IMPACT* and *eclipse*, two award-winning publications based in New Orleans. He has been called upon by the local news media, as well as TV and radio personalities, to represent his views on various topics.

He has taught at the post-secondary level for over twenty-five years, and he has been a keynote speaker or primary presenter at conferences, churches, and university classrooms.

This is his second work of fiction. His first novel, *Angel on My Corner*, was published in 2019.

www.ingramcontent.com/pod-product-compliance
Lightning Source LLC
Chambersburg PA
CBHW030745110726
47900CB00008B/2461